CITY OF THE LOST

BOOK THREE OF THE AWAKENING WARS

William H. Nelson

BOOKS BY WILLIAM H. NELSON

<u>The Awakening Wars Series:</u>

Within the Range of Reanimation
The Unnamed Town
City of the Lost
The Sacred Cenote (upcoming)
The Dagger of Azazil (upcoming)

<u>Other Novels:</u>
Nathrotep
The Loathing

ACKNOWLEDGEMENTS

They say it takes a village, and with this new novel that was certainly true. I would like to thank all my editors for their invaluable assistance in helping me to iron out the kinks in the story; T.J. Tranchell, Eris Hyrkas, (who is also my cousin from Minnesota), and all the good folks over at EbookPbook. In addition, publishing this book would not have been possible without the linguistic aide from my language consultants; Ron "Qiilu" Panigeo and Maryland "Aviuk" Panigeo for the Inuit dialogue, and Yuridia Henry for the Spanish. Also, I would like to thank Al Landron for allowing me to use one of his amazing sculptures for the center piece on the cover. His other works can be found at landronartifacts.etsy.com. And lastly, my dear readers, it is you who I would like to thank most of all. Without your ongoing support these stories would never see the light of day, and so I humbly offer my sincere gratitude for your continued readership. Thank you all so very much!

PROLOGUE

Director Anne Wilkenson

"Alpha team leader, report back to base command," I instructed through the transceiver for the third time that day. "And that's an order!"

Charles DeCovney gave me a sidelong glance as I handed him back the microphone, an unspoken question hanging between us. It made my shoulder blades itch to see that look in his eyes, his curious gaze lingering on me with forthright consideration, watching me like a lab tech waiting to see if a mouse will make it to the end of the maze. Studiously ignoring him, I walked back over to the chart table, trying, almost successfully, to look like I knew what I was doing. But so far, this whole operation had been a nightmare, filled with one failure after another. We could barely catch a break in this case and seemed always just one step behind those Alaskan hunters we'd followed halfway across the country.

Now we were stuck in a backwater province on the outskirts of Arizona, a pissant little ghost town that was only the first in a whole string of failed communities dotting the landscape. Places like this always gave me the creeps, and the ones in this area were no exception. They had all somehow been systematically destroyed from within, succumbing, one after the other, to a tragic, unknown fate that, so far, we'd been unable to fathom. But after we'd arrived, I'd quickly discovered that this particular town also had a dark and sinister past. And its unusual history was well known, at least to my superiors.

Although it was no longer featured on any map, it had once been called Plentsville. This was way before my time, but the dossier lying open on the table as I sat down gave me all the info I needed. There'd been an uprising of sorts about thirty years ago, something to do with a cult leader and his shadowy minions. The cabal had been put down, but its taint still remained. I had only to raise my eyes, gaze at the piled bodies stacked beyond the open tent flap, and breathe in the sharp, pungent aroma of ripening death to remind myself what sort of legacy their sorcerous deeds had left behind. This infestation had to have been something cooked up by their occult meddling, and it wasn't pretty.

Leaning back in the uncomfortable chair, I stretched my neck from side to side, trying to relieve some of the tension and stiffness. *How the hell did we wind up on cleanup duty again anyway?* I wondered, already knowing the answer. And following those rat bastards hadn't been a cakewalk either.

The aunt had given us nothing to go on, but by placing a watch on all routes out of Anchorage, I'd been able to discover that our two fugitives had stowed away on a cargo vessel heading for Washington State. From there, it had been a simple enough matter to track the boat and put eyes and ears on the ground at their destination. Yet, somehow, they'd still managed to slip through our grasp, and it had taken a considerable amount of effort for us to pick up their trail again.

A lucky break from a traffic cam image had revealed they were on the move, this time in a sleek black sedan, heading south. Everyone had assumed they were making for the border, perhaps even trying a run down to Mexico, but I'd known better. No, these boys were smarter than that. They knew we'd pick them off easily at the crossing. So I'd had my team dig into the background of our main suspect's deceased uncle—and low and behold—there were dozens of his old business associates scattered all across the globe. By a process of elimination and deduction, I was able to narrow it down to those few who were low profile enough to offer my little escapees aid. And the name that had floated to the tippy-top of that very short list had been Jarrod Thibodeaux, resident of this blighted community and a dabbler in the occult arts. We'd already been well on our way to this godforsaken place when the new reports had started pouring in.

Glancing down at the map, I moved aside a cold cup of coffee, leaving a dark ring staining the upper corner. The dots indicating towns were clustered together and now had concentric, vaguely circular outlines in varying colors, denoting things like depths and concavity. It would appear that shortly after our fugitives had arrived, there'd been some sort of underground upheaval. No one yet knew the exact dimensions of this immense seismic event, but much like the results of a sinkhole forming, all these towns had settled into the ground as if a subterranean bubble had suddenly burst beneath them. And there were so many of them that I was stunned by the implications. Who could have guessed there would be dozens of deserted communities out here that were seemingly interconnected? Once they'd been removed from any existing maps, no one really kept track anymore, so they'd just completely fallen off the radar.

What exactly had happened here, and more importantly, what had happened to the townsfolk? My eyes rose once more to stare out over the piles of dead monstrosities my team had been stacking up all day, grimacing at the dark images suddenly floating through my overimaginative mind. If what I surmised were true, then they never even had a chance. This overabundance of voracious, carnivorous creatures, a subhuman race that was only partially known to us, told me all I needed to know about the whereabouts of the missing townsfolk. And it was not pleasant to dwell on the terror they must have felt, envision their unnecessarily painful deaths. The very thought of it sickened me.

To add insult to injury, our suspects had given us the slip yet again. Without any way to track them unless we could get a bead on their vehicle via satellite, they could be anywhere by now. And much like what had happened up in the Brooks Range, it appeared that we'd once more arrived just in time to clean up after them. In my mind, it was a surety that this whole shitstorm was somehow tied to their visit here in some way. I heard my knuckles crack and glanced down, realizing I'd been clenching my fists in frustration. Wherever these boys were hiding, whatever they knew or thought they knew, I was going to find them, and I was going to obtain that information by any means necessary. They were in for a whole world of hurt, and that was an understatement.

But first, I had to deal with the problems that had arisen under my own command.

By my estimation, the leadership skills I possessed were never in doubt. But this opinion was not shared by over half my team, or so it would seem. As my mind turned to these internal problems, Andrew Hillman and his band of cronies sauntered into the tent, laughing and smiling like a bunch of unruly schoolboys who'd just pulled off the world's greatest prank. Think of the devil and the devil appears, and in this case, he was in the form of this self-important asshat who thought he could just skate around my orders without any fear of retribution. Straightening my shoulders, I prepared to give this preening little fucktard a dressing down he would not soon forget.

"Alpha team," he said, sweeping into a mock bow and theatrically extending an arm to include the group of men gathered behind him, "reporting as ordered, *sir!*"

I sat back and studied him for a long moment, letting the coldness of my displeasure fill the tent like an arctic gale. And the prick just stared right back, that little grin of his quirking at the edges of his mouth as he awaited my reply. This nihilistic jackass thought he was all that and a bucket of hot wings. Seeing him standing there in all his trumped-up glory, I had to admit that he certainly had the looks to pull it off, with his wavy blond hair, blue eyes, and meticulously trimmed mustache. Somewhat lacking in the brains department, though.

I stared him down, letting the silence drag on until his men began to shift around uncomfortably. "Exactly what part of reporting back in on time," I finally asked, "especially in the middle of an important operation, are you not getting, Agent Hillman?"

"*Important operation?*" he exclaimed. "I'd hardly call this low-level CHUD hunt an 'operation'." Smiling, he pointed outside the tent to the growing pile of malformed dead. "In fact, I'd say I wrapped up this so-called 'operation' hours ago and delivered it to your front doorstep, all tied up in a pretty little bow."

Cute. He was using B horror movie references to describe the carnivorous lifeforms he'd almost entirely wiped out against my direct orders. They were indeed 'cannibalistic humanoid underground dwellers' but of a type and population density that we'd never before encountered. And now, thanks to him, we'd probably never determine the true origins of this unusual pack or the reason they were even here in the first place. Not to mention the whereabouts of our missing suspects.

"Your orders were to secure the area and then lead a squad into the tunnels to sweep for evidence," I said. "Not destroy the nest and set charges to blow up the rest of the den before we had a chance to investigate. Your dereliction of duty has hindered our ability to solve this case and undermined my authority. And we still have no idea where our witnesses have gotten off to or if they're even still alive at all."

There. Let him chew on that for a minute. But he was having none of it. Bristling, he straightened to his full height, towering over me in righteous indignation.

"I followed your orders to the letter, *Director*," he grated out. "The area has been secured. And if I hadn't set those charges, our position would now be overrun. The ground-penetrating radar clearly showed a buildup of additional forces back in the deepest parts of those tunnels. I found it necessary to protect our men by taking steps to make sure they couldn't come at us all at once. Now, they'll have to disperse to other exits and approach our position in much smaller groups if they still want to attack. I have men out looking for these other access points, and our eye in the sky is doing round-the-clock surveillance. If it wasn't for me, we could all be dead by now! If you had more experience, then maybe you would have thought of these things yourself instead of staying in the command tent and letting others do your job for you."

He was way out of line. But pointing out that I'd thought of all that and had taken the necessary precautions would seem shrewish of me. The men already mistrusted my leadership. In this cavalier idiot, they saw a better choice, someone with more experience, who had enough personal magnetism to gather loyalty and devotion with little effort. Someone they already looked up to. But fuck that; this was my show, and I'd be damned if I was going to let this chode-swallowing orangutan ruin it for me.

I opened my mouth to let him have it but was interrupted by one of my scouts bursting into the tent.

"Sorry for the intrusion, ma'am," she said, nervously glancing around at the other senior agents. "But we found that shop you were looking for. Our perps were there, alright, but they must have cleared out just in the last few hours. From the skid marks left in the road out front, it looks like they were in a hurry. I've put some men on it and should be able to get you a fix on them shortly. Also, those other exits you asked us to find have all been identified. We have teams standing by, awaiting orders on how you'd like us to proceed. Is this a tag 'em and bag 'em, or do you want trackers attached to a sample of the population as they come to the surface?"

Well, well. At least someone was following orders. This was good news; if we could get a bead on our Alaskan hunters, we could have them in custody by the end of the day. And the higher-ups really wanted to know where all of these subhuman creatures were coming from, what they were doing here, and how we could deal with them quietly without endangering the rest of the population. Glancing down at the maps, I could not help but realize what an enormous undertaking this was going to turn into. We could be here for days cleaning it all up.

And if it hadn't been for this asshole and his sycophants, I could have had the creatures rounded up en masse when they came to the surface from the main exit point. My plan had always been to hold them in one place, not scatter them into the deeper tunnels like this vacuous moron had done. I had to address his insubordination, but now seemed like bad timing. He had all of these men with him, and dismissing them to take him down a few pegs in private would only strengthen their resentment of me. Trying not to sigh, I glared at him, judging how far I could even trust him at this point. No matter what happened next, he was undeniably popular and an adequate if not overly bright field agent. I decided to utilize him where he could do no further harm, thereby getting him out of my hair for the time being while I took care of our real objectives. Sure, it was a bit of a cop-out, but it was the best I could do for now without ruffling anyone's feathers.

"From here on out," I told him, "you are to run all your ideas by me before you implement them. Is that understood?"

He scowled at my tone but answered readily enough with a sullen, "Yes, sir."

"Now, take your men and get those other exits secured. I need a sample of the population tagged and released, then you can mop up the rest. The higher-ups want to know where this outbreak originated and how best to contain it. So get out there and get it done. Dismissed!"

With an exasperated huff, he left the tent, the others following doggedly at his heels. The scout looked at me, studiously ignoring what had just transpired while awaiting further orders. I decided that I just might have to give her a promotion. Glancing over, I caught Agent DeCovney staring at me again with that reproachful look in his eyes.

"*What?*" I barked, daring him to comment.

Turning away, he busied himself at the radio controls, funneling queries and orders through the communication channels of our busy command center. *Yeah, that's what I thought.* Composing myself, I got back to work, ready to give new directives to my scout before refocusing on our main objective: finding and questioning the hunters who had slipped through our fingers since that debacle up in the Brooks Range.

1

Gillam

Settling into the uncomfortable crew seat in the back cargo area of the Boeing 767, I tried to ease my cramping muscles while agonizing over the decisions I'd made in the last few hours. We'd barely escaped with our lives from the unnamed town, and it had taken all of our combined skills, not to mention a considerable amount of luck, to thwart Nathrotep's plans before fleeing the area. It was an uncharitable thought, but if it weren't for the fact that I currently needed them both, I might have already strangled my two companions along the way. Between Jarrod's strong hatred for the spirit now inhabiting Tunuhun's body and that same spirit's scathing bouts of lucidity whenever he managed to emerge, I'd been spending a lot of my time keeping them from killing each other. Even though Tunuhun was growing stronger by the minute and was able to resist the spirit's control 98 percent of the time, Jarrod still took every opportunity to berate him, always trying to find a crack in his burgeoning willpower. The whole situation was giving me a migraine.

But if it had not been for Jarrod and my uncle's journal, we wouldn't have even made it this far. Fortunately, the fat shopkeeper knew people in the shipping business from his years spent handling collectibles from around the world. After calling in a few favors, we'd wound up disguised as freight haulers aboard a cargo flight out of Phoenix, heading to Lima, Peru. It was there that he said we'd find help in translating the stone map tile fragment, and my uncle's journal seemed to confirm it. But we were still on the run from government agents and desperately needed to perform a ritual that would drive the undead warlock from Tunuhun's body. Right before we left, Jarrod had suddenly decided that he'd be willing to attempt the exorcism on his own, and my decision to put it off until we were safely away from American soil had not been a popular one.

The notes left by my late uncle spoke of a colleague who'd spent a lifetime translating dead languages and discovering the meanings behind obscure relics found in isolated corners of the world. He was a renowned archaeologist and appeared to have been one of my uncle's most trusted associates. Armed with this knowledge, I'd done a simple internet search and verified that he was still in Peru; apparently there'd been another ancient city found deep in jungles there. Much like Machu Picchu, these ruins were thought to be one of the missing refuges of the Incas as they fled persecution by the Spaniards back in the 1500s. It was not believed to be the fabled lost city of gold but perhaps one of their other trading outposts that had remained hidden in the depths of the Amazon until its recent discovery.

According to the information I'd read online, the archaeologist's base of operations was located in downtown Lima. It wasn't much to go on, but at least it was a start. I just hoped this Dr. Octavious Huxtable would be able to assist with the translations, perhaps even point us in the right direction. We had to find the rest of the map tile fragments, or even an undamaged version of the whole pictographic slab, in order to locate more of the ancient Mi-Go bases. Our goal was to uncover enough alien technology to potentially fight off their impending invasion while also discovering a means to further disrupt Nathrotep's plans. We may have set him back by destabilizing his interdimensional ghoul city, but there was no doubt in my mind that the self-proclaimed demigod would continue toward his ultimate goal of enslaving the entire planet. It was this assortment of worrisome thoughts that continuously swirled through my mind as I leaned back and closed my eyes, eventually lulled into a fitful slumber by the dull roar of the 767's engines.

Sensations stirred me back to awareness; the sudden pressure of millions of gallons of water pressing against me on all sides, the strong push and pull of the currents as they rippled across my turgid body, and the clouds of infinitesimal organisms mixing with the silt rushing past as it flowed over my outstretched membranous wings. Ahead, on the bottom of the dark abyss, my ocular cilia detected the megalithic remains of ruined architecture, a location that had once been the sister city to a larger metropolis residing just beyond the mountains of the tropical southern pole. What had happened here? To what cataclysmic event did I attribute this destruction of my ancestral home?

This maelstrom of sensory input, experienced as if it were my own thoughts and perceptions, was familiar yet entirely alien in nature, and I realized that I must be dreaming. Or perhaps my psychic link to the being Jarrod had called an 'Elder Thing' was allowing me to share this glimpse into the mind of the creature we'd released from Mi-Go captivity up in the Brooks Range. Whatever the source of these peculiar sensations and images, I knew I was not fully in control. As it glided through the murky depths, its brethren fanning out to either side, I could feel the uneasiness that was shared by them all.

This could not be the place they sought, and yet somehow, it was. Propelling themselves swiftly through the pitch-black, salt-saturated liquid, these entities used their natural ability to see across almost limitless spectrums. Thus, they were able to view this shadowy aquatic ecosystem with full clarity using the prismatic cilia, which served them as eyes. But this once-familiar region had changed somehow. A memory surfaced— gliding through these same waters when it was younger, feeling the warmth of the currents flowing across its pebbly outer hide. Yet the temperatures here were now bitterly cold, like the sensation of flying through deep space had been when its ancient race had traveled here so long ago. *How can this be?* It seemed to consider, its alien thoughts projected as a series of conceptual imagery.

Just how long had we been held captive by our sworn enemies? Letting those concerns go for now, it streaked through the freezing currents, heading for the jumbled stone monuments lying collapsed and broken in the silt-ridden muck below us.

As the rest of its companions spread out, searching for any signs of habitation, the Elder Thing considered the moldering ruins. Much of it was still familiar—here were the remains of a building that had once housed the center of commerce, while over there lay the remnants of the science ministry. But all was in shambles now, laid to waste by some unknown catastrophe. Before it could come to any satisfactory conclusions about the cause of such destruction, its brethren had ended their fruitless search, gathering in the central, star-shaped amphitheater to decide on their next course of action.

I could see now that there were hundreds of them, all of the captive Elder Things that had been locked in stasis tubes when we'd investigated the diabolical upper rooms of the Mi-Go hive. They gathered together, their rotund bodies gliding through the water to settle around their leader, the branching tentacles which served them as arms waving in intricate patterns. With their starfish-shaped heads and ovular appearance, they reminded me of a vast carpet of overgrown sea anemones, their appendages drifting hypnotically with the currents and creating a spectacle of writhing tubular motion. And while riding the perceptions of my unsuspecting host, I could somewhat understand their speech patterns, comprehend their communications as they met there below the waves of the cold southern sea. Some thought they should vacate the area, try to make contact with other places where their race had once flourished. Others put forth the idea of traveling above to visit the larger metropolis first. A few even suggested that they leave the planet entirely.

But the creature I inhabited was unsure. There was something vastly wrong here, something that had to do with the smaller lifeforms who'd helped them escape. As the images that served as its thought processes considered me, it suddenly recognized my presence intertwined within its five-lobed brain. Once it became aware of me, it began listening to my own thoughts in return, reaching out toward my subconscious mind while seeking to communicate more fully. I realized then that it was getting harder for us to separate from one another, the bond we'd formed in the Mi-Go torture chamber becoming stronger, allowing us to better comprehend each other's strange and entirely alien ideologies. The main thing it could immediately deduce from sharing my perceptions was that its enemies were still alive and it was now trapped in an unfamiliar age. Somehow, an extraordinary length of time had passed as it had lain frozen in stasis, held captive by the insect-like Mi-Go and forced into experimental modification. Intrigued by the information it was receiving, it began riffling through my memories, attempting to learn more.

Sometime during this sharing of discordant thoughts and ideas, something stirred in the ruins around us, interrupting the exchange. Viewing our surroundings through its sensory nodules, it witnessed colossal blocks of stone and broken segments of once carefully planned monuments heaving upward from the seabed as beings of a dark and sinister nature made themselves known. From out of the murky depths there came a bone-chilling cry, a nightmarish sound that should never have been voiced. *Where had these underlings been hiding, and who were their keepers?* The image-thoughts came to me. *Who has unleashed these slaves to do so as they please, to threaten us without fear of censure or retribution?* Peering across the amphitheater through its multiple eyestalks, it discovered we were now completely surrounded, hemmed in by seething amoeba-like entities who held no shape nor form, only limitless variations. These were smaller and underdeveloped, but I recognized them as well. They were obviously kin to the protoplasmic creature we'd seen attacking the Mi-Go right before their foul base had exploded.

From the convoluted creases of the barrel-shaped being's complex brain there arose an idea, an image coached in time, born from the very bowels of an ancient past. It was a name, perhaps, maybe even a title, but it put a sound, an image, a word to the ultimate horror of demented destruction that was now preparing to attack:

Shoggoth.

These were the remnants of its bioengineered slave race, the beasts of burden that had once helped raise great cities all across this primordial world they'd found here on the fringes of interstellar space. Seeing the imminent danger, the Elder Thing's brethren closed ranks on all sides, brandishing the weapons they'd regained from their enemy's stronghold during the escape. As they formed into a classic, five-pointed defense configuration, the army of feral shoggoths surged through the water, expanding and evolving as they advanced.

It was a startling collection of tentacles, pincers, eyestalks, and crab-like legs that the Elder Things now faced. And although each of their enemies was an individual, they had joined to form a gigantic, constricting ring of interconnected, protoplasmic tissues. As I watched through the sensory organs of my alien counterpart, they flowed forward, pieces of broken architecture and clouds of silt rising before them, fouling the waters with a floating particulated sludge. It was madness incarnate, and I recoiled from the horror of it all, hoping to wake from what had now become a fever dream of unlimited terror. While the shoggoths boiled forth from the cracks and crevasses of the ruined underwater city, forming a great wall of ever-changing flesh that swiftly closed in on us from all sides, I squirmed within the Elder Thing's mind, trying desperately to break myself free.

Yet the creature whose thoughts I shared was stoic in the face of such adversity. It assessed the situation with a degree of calm assurance that I envied and then formulated a strategy to rebuff the impending assault. I could sense its lower five appendages, much like a starfish's arms, anchoring themselves into the broken stone beneath us, feel its five membranous wings fanning as if to steady itself in the strong oceanic currents, stabilizing its rotund body as it readied for battle. It was reaching outward with all of its many senses, the ocular nodules at the ends of its star-shaped head perceiving spectrums of light and shadow that I could only dream of, viewing its adversaries and sizing them up accordingly. Then, with a slow precision that the hunter in me admired, it readied its weapon, preparing to shatter the cohesion of its enemy's amalgamated attack.

But just as it was about to fire upon the encircling wall of oncoming protoplasm, the startling reverberations of a deep, groaning ululation echoed out through the surrounding waters.

Rolling to a stop, the shoggoths ceased their forward momentum, pulsating in confusion as clouds of silt and other debris settled slowly around them. They seemed to be considering something, perhaps waiting, somehow communing with one another. Just as they looked to have decided to continue their combined offensive, another haunting call rippled through the oceanic depths, freezing them in place before they could resume their aggressive advance.

I had no idea what horrific and unknown behemoth could have made those moaning, deeply disturbing cries. Here, many fathoms beneath the surface of the sea in the most isolated part of the world, there were not many creatures that could have produced such an unearthly sound. And yet, sound it was, even though for me it was more like a series of reverberations traveling through thousands of gallons of pressurized water, impacting against the sensory organs of the being I was currently inhabiting. If this were only a dream, then it was one born from the hidden recesses of my innermost fears. For as I watched on, sharing the Elder Thing's perceptions, the water above us began to grow even darker.

How could that be? How could this lightless aquatic world suddenly become even more shadowed than it had previously been just moments before? Seeing through the Elder Thing's ocular cilia, this difference in the tonal quality of its perceived visual spectrum was startling to behold. It was as if some legendary beast dredged up out of the annals of ancient seafaring lore was moving into place above us, overshadowing the sunken ruins with the bulk of its enormous body.

The tension its presence created was palpable. Hundreds of Elder Things, locked together in the middle of a protective star-shaped formation, readied their weapons, while around them in the ruination of the ancient city, the rebellious shoggoths writhed and gibbered in mounting hysteria. This formless race of bioengineered slaves must have lain dormant here for many thousands of years, waiting for another chance to smite the cruel masters they'd risen against so long ago. But even in their current state of murderous delirium, they still cowered like terrified children before the might of the being above us.

Currents shifted, the titanic pressures of the deep now amplified and squeezing with immeasurable force as this monstrous lifeform began to descend, becoming more and more visible. Yet its form was so vast that its true identity remained incomprehensible, a great expanse of indistinct, mottled flesh stretching as far as the eye could see in all directions. As it came closer, bioluminescent patches, like those found only in deep sea organisms, flickered to life within it, painting the landscape in dull splotches of fluorescent color which only served to further illustrate the immensity of its tremendous size.

In response, the shoggoths continued to recoil, bubbling and flowing one into the other, changing from moment to moment as they writhed away from the descending threat. Then, through the murky darkness, there came another vocalization, this one so loud it was deafening, a great, burbling cry so resonant that it would have shattered the eardrums of any lesser being. When the rippling vibrations of this undulating roar hit the Elder Thing full-on, my mind fractured beneath its oscillating repercussions, and I was blasted clear of our mental joining. Floating free of the creature's five-lobed brain at last, my astral form began to dissolve, the pieces of my tattered lifeforce streaming away into the currents around us.

I realized then that this was not entirely a dream. Somehow, my spiritual essence had been drawn out of me as I slumbered, my soul captured within the thoughts and actions of the Elder Thing with whom I'd formed such a cohesive mental bond. And now, it was too late to find a way back to my own physical body. Not only was it thousands of miles away, but I could already feel that the tenuous psychic connection leading back to it was beginning to fray. As I continued to helplessly dematerialize, the creatures around me readied themselves for battle, the being above them descending more rapidly as it bellowed out yet another bellicose challenge.

But there was something else I could sense now as well, another presence that my fading intellect could suddenly discern only on the edges of reality as my consciousness flowed steadily away into the frigid waters. It was larger than us all, a power so deep and vast that I could scarcely comprehend it. But in my current state of expanding awareness, I could feel it watching us, observing all that transpired within those benighted alien ruins sunken deep below the surface of the cold southern sea. And as I continued to slowly unravel, despair overtaking me, I felt this presence reach out, enveloping the remaining pieces of my envanishing soul.

This was insanity! Could it be that I was becoming delusional here at the end of my life, utterly losing myself to madness as I drifted closer to my own impending demise? But without hesitation, this mysterious being had collected up the fragments of my disintegrating lifeforce, somehow weaving them back together before hauling me through the intervening miles and then redepositing me into the cargo area of the Boeing 767. As my reconstructed spirit settled back down into my still slumbering body, I was thankful to feel the straps once more securing my physical form to the uncomfortable seat.

"If you wish to discover the answers you seek," a warm, somewhat feminine voice whispered within the confines of my subconscious mind, "do not attempt such an unskilled astral projection again. Come find me within the realms of dream instead, and there you will learn all that you need to know."

With that final admonishment, the enigmatic presence was gone, and I sank gratefully into a once more peaceful slumber, no longer troubled by visions of that distant aquatic conflict.

2

I awoke just as the plane touched down, but it didn't feel like I'd even truly rested at all. As we disembarked, we were offered a lift by one of the pilot's employees, and I settled into an even deeper gloom than before. Fortunately, my two companions seemed to have called an uneasy truce, probably the result of jet lag more than anything else. Whatever it was, they were both blissfully silent as we sped through the city in an old, battered Volvo.

The things I'd experienced during the previous night were weighing heavily upon me; what did it all mean, and was any of it real or just a figment of my overactive imagination? But try as I might, I just couldn't get the images of what had transpired in those moldering oceanic ruins out of my mind. The Elder Things readying for battle, the attack of those feral shoggoths, and the even greater threat descending from above—it seemed so unreal. Yet there was an undeniable lucidity to it all, as if I'd actually been transported to another plane of existence, somewhere these fantastical events were a reality instead of vivid nightmare. And just who was that otherworldly presence that had pulled me out right at the last second? Without her help, would I have actually died, my spiritual essence left to unravel into nothingness there at the bottom of the cold southern sea? Shaking my head to clear the disturbing memories from my mind, I attempted to center myself in the here and now, focusing on the sights and sounds of the city we were currently traversing.

The original Spanish settlers had constructed their buildings modeled after the Andalusian designs familiar to them from their hometown of Seville, back in Spain. This architectural style, influenced by Roman and Islamic techniques, featured the use of high arches, towering spires, and grand colonnades. The results were stunning, and unlike Nathrotep's darkly Gothic aesthetic, the edifices here often featured unique additions painted in bright, warm colors. Everywhere I looked, there were wondrous sights to behold, the mixture of old-world charm and modern-day embellishments blending together into a breathtaking, picture-perfect whole. Palm trees and a glorious fountain graced the Plaza de Armas as we pulled up, where crowds of citizens were walking along on various errands, enjoying the sun and the windblown mist coming off the beautifully sculpted waterworks. It was a welcome sight to see such splendor after experiencing so much darkness and despair.

Even as tired as I was, I couldn't help but smile as the driver dropped us off and we walked the remaining distance from the governor's palace to my uncle's safe house, which was nestled in a row of other mansions of similar quality. Its proportions were extravagant, to say the least, standing four stories tall with colonnaded balconies and arched stonework decorating the entirety of its yellow and white painted facade. Following the directions on his tablet, we made our way through an alley running along the right side and then around to a back set of stairs leading down.

This part of Lima was less populated and tucked away from the heavier foot traffic of the central square. It seemed to be a neighborhood that was mostly forgotten about, except by the wealthy owners of its various other grandiose homes. So we went entirely unnoticed as we used the electronic keypad to let ourselves into the subbasement level.

The room we found ourselves in was small and utilitarian, basically just a secure area guarding an elevator. Climbing into the waiting conveyance, we hit the button for the next level up, then waited for the carriage to arrive at our destination. By now, I was so weary from overcoming the many obstacles we'd faced over the last few days that I was hoping to be able to refresh myself before contacting Huxtable.

But once the doors slid open, we stepped out into a sumptuous foyer that took my breath away. It featured a grand central staircase leading up to a mezzanine that split the remaining stairs to either side. And behind this first landing was a large, three-sided window embrasure, almost like a turret, faced with elaborately designed stained-glass windows. The light streaming in through these elegant panes spread in multicolored patterns across the floor, flowing across the decorative tilework and then up the walls to illuminate the exquisitely done oil paintings hanging there.

The stylized decor of this room relied heavily upon geometric and arabesque motifs done in wood, stucco, and tile. Everywhere I looked, there were patterns sculpted, molded, or painstakingly created, using differing types of complementary materials. Four towering archways led to other parts of the home, and the elaborately carved front doors, which were barred from the outside, were situated just to the left. As I stepped forward into this impressive-looking entrance hall, I took it all in, marveling at the range of exotic materials and fine woodwork used throughout. I suppose the architectural splendor of the place was fitting given that my uncle had been a collector of so many rare and wondrous artifacts, yet I still could not help but admire the beauty all around us.

"Let's get cleaned up," I said after a moment of deep appreciation. "According to my uncle's notes, there should be four bathrooms upstairs. Pick one and grab a shower. We'll contact Huxtable afterward to see about showing him the map tile fragment."

Jarrod had wandered a bit and was currently gazing up at one of the paintings on the far wall. After hearing of my intentions, he spun toward me, his face turning beet red as his mouth gaped open in shock. Dropping the heavy bags he carried, he advanced on me like a locomotive with a full head of steam.

"What we outta to do right now is *perform the exorcism!*" he said, poking his rigid index finger into my chest for emphasis. "The longer that warlock remains insida him, the harder it's gonna be to banish it!"

He wasn't wrong, but now was not the time; I was so wiped out I could barely even think straight. Our escape from the Mi-Go hive, our inadvertent encounter with Nathrotep and his hybrid ghoul legions, and then our hours-long flight to Peru—all of it had worn me ragged. Right now what I really needed was a hot shower and then some decent food that hadn't been bought at a gas station mini-mart. Turning to look over at Tunuhun, I tried to ascertain if Ezra was currently in control or not, but it was hard to be certain. My companion's face was as impassive as ever, the same serene yet intelligent expression that he always wore.

"How are you holding up?" I asked. "Are you . . . *you* right now?"

He considered the question, then nodded. "Aŋatkuq siquruq."

"Whatever excuse he done gave you just ain't good enough!" Jarrod cut in. "We don't have no way a tellin' if he's in control or not; Ezra could be runnin' the show right now, and we'd never even know the difference! We gotta get that damn thing outta him, and we gotta do it *now!*"

"But you said the ritual will take time to prepare," I pointed out, "and also warned us how dangerous it could be. As long as Tunuhun is himself, I'm certain he can hold the warlock at bay while we focus on gathering the necessary components you'll need to safely perform the ritual. Right now, he says the spirit is asleep, so there's no sense in rushing things. Let's not go off half-cocked—I don't want anyone getting killed during the process."

"Worryin' about whether we's gonna get kilt or not is a waste of time!" he fumed. "Iffen we don't do somethin' soon, that sonovabitch is gonna wipe us all out anyways.

Best to destroy him now, no matter the cost, afore he can use them dark powers again us!"

"Look, you've already told us he'd normally only be able to take over weak-minded individuals or those who'd offered themselves up willingly. In fact, you claimed he doesn't yet have enough power to completely overcome someone who's mentally and physically fit. Tunuhun is one of the strongest people I know; surely we can trust that he has the situation well in hand, at least for now?"

"I wouldn't hang my hat on it," Jarrod scoffed, his bloodshot eyes narrowing as he favored Tunuhun with a look of pure loathing. "Ezra's most likely just bidin' his time in there, plannin' to strike once we's lulled into a false sense a security!"

I gazed at my stalwart companion, studying him while trying to gauge his reaction. And he just stared right back, his dark eyes meeting my own with a placid expression of wholehearted trust. I was still in command here, and it was up to me to decide, for better or for worse.

"Are you sure you're alright?" I asked again, hoping for a more definite indication that he was currently free from the spirit's manipulations.

"Aŋatkuq nipaitchuq," he stated quietly, reassuring me that the spirit was currently quiescent.

"Why don't you just say what you gotta say in plain English, you rat bastard!" Jarrod exploded. "I don't wanna hear no more of that gooky-soundin' foreign talk! He's in there, lurkin' just below the surface—I can feel it! And I aim to banish him back to hell iffen it's the last thing I do!"

This level of aggression was abnormal, even when coming from the unbalanced shopkeeper. His state of mind, never overly stable to begin with, seemed filled with rage whenever he thought about the person this dark spirit had once been. There was a history there, and one going back many years. Yet, even so, there was no call for this kind of racially biased hate speech. I glanced at Tunuhun, watching him closely. His expression hadn't changed, yet there was an undeniable quality to the sudden glint in his eyes. Turning away from me, he took a careful step toward Jarrod, outwardly calm but studying the portly man with a hunter's calculating assessment of unsuspecting prey. Stepping in between them, I put a hand on his chest, stopping his advance and warning him off with a shake of my head. He took a deep breath, exhaled it slowly, and then nodded, backing down.

When would I ever be able to catch a break with these two? Their arguing, although mostly one-sided while the spirit lay dormant, was really starting to piss me off. We had other things to worry about right now, bigger things! Yes, the ritual was important, and freeing my friend from possession was clearly high on my list of things to do. But this naked animosity between them just had to stop. I couldn't take it anymore!

"Enough!" I exclaimed, rounding on Jarrod. "Will you just give it a fucking rest already! I'm sick to death of hearing it! The warlock is trapped inside him, and we do need to exorcise it as soon as possible, but that isn't going to happen right this second, and especially not with you being such an ass about it! If Tunuhun says he's got it handled, then you can believe it! Besides, the spirit needs us right now; by his own admission Ezra has to have our willing cooperation in order to strike back at Nathrotep. So, for the time being, we need to focus on getting this artifact translated and then find a way to stop the Mi-Go invasion! We don't need you carping at us all day long. We already know how deep in the shit we are right now, so you constantly bitching about it isn't going to change anything!"

The man stood there a moment, his eyes protruding in shock. Then his face flared an even brighter shade of red. "You just ain't understandin' the level of danger we's in right now!" he raged. "That spirit is the devil incarnate! Iffen we don't do somethin' soon, he'll find a way to take total control, whether you likes it or not! An' once that happens, do you really think he's gonna wanna work with us, be part a whatever the hell this is?" His hand swiveled in a circle, including us all in the limp-wristed gesture. "Imma tellin' you, the longer we keep puttin' it off, the deeper his hold will grow, festerin' inside 'til there ain't nothin' left in there but *him*! Your friend might be the strongest person you know right now, but is he stronger than an undead warlock who knows alla them ancient spells contained in this here book? I don't think so! So pull your head outta your goddamn ass and help me get things ready! Or I can guarantee that you won't live to regret it!"

Clenching my fists, I closed my eyes for a brief moment, trying to regain some sense of equilibrium. But the anger and frustration had already blown itself out; now all I felt was exhaustion and shame. Jarrod had a point. And what did I truly know about demonic possession anyway? Or even Ezra Jedidiah himself, for that matter? The short answer was almost nothing at all.

It suddenly struck me that if Jarrod was saying we needed to do this ritual right now, then he was saying it because he was deeply afraid. And the more I thought about that simple fact, the more my own anxiety grew.

"Listen," I said, "you're right. And I apologize for my outburst. But we need to work together instead of constantly bickering. Why don't you get everything prepared while Tunuhun and I seek out Dr. Huxtable? Then, when we get back, I'll help you in any way I can. But keep in mind that I won't allow you to harm my friend just for the sake of your own petty vengeance. Whatever esoteric procedure you come up with, it better have a safety net."

The man's anger drained away immediately as he sighed in heartfelt relief. Reaching up to scratch at his stubbly double chin, he considered the problem with a calculating look crossing his flabby features. "There are a number of ways we can make it less dangerous, now that you mention it. An' that just might make it more effective as well. These things always tend to work out better iffen the subject is cooperative, an' I can tell that your friend there is willin'." Turning away, he shuffled back over to his bags, bending to root through them while apparently forgetting we were even still there at all.

Watching him gather together the occult paraphernalia we needed, I silently wondered what I'd gotten myself into when I'd decided to work with this temperamental old man. But the dice had been cast, and we were stuck with the results. At least for now. Besides, regardless of his idiosyncrasies, the knowledge and experience he possessed were necessary for the success of all our future plans. Shaking my head, I decided to let him sort out the details; I was in no shape for such mental calisthenics. Glancing back at my friend, I motioned him toward the upper levels. "Let's go get cleaned up and then find something to eat," I said. "We'll deal with Ezra later."

Nodding in that unassuming way he had of accepting all my decisions, he turned toward the stairs, completely confident in my grasp of the situation. I only wished I were as confident in it myself. As I began to follow, I put my worries aside, dreaming only of the hot shower awaiting me. But then he suddenly stopped, giving me the hand signal to do likewise as he peered up into the shadows residing above the second-story landing.

Pausing mid-step, I took his cue as seriously as I would have if we were out on a hunt. His eyes, bathed in the colored light shining in from the stained-glass windows, searched the upper balustrades, his face taut with concentration. It was a look I knew only too well—he sensed danger and was trying to determine the source of it. As I eased myself into a more defensive posture, I heard the unmistakable metallic *snick* of a gun being cocked somewhere above. It was all the warning I needed, but before I could take any decisive action, a voice echoed down from beyond the third-floor balcony.

"No te muevas! Que estas haciendo aqui?"

We were powerless to resist since we hadn't yet gathered any weapons from my uncle's stash. And even though it had been years since I'd studied Spanish, the words were familiar enough—a command to stand your ground in any language is easily understood. Raising our hands, we searched the balconies above us, trying to deduce the source of this forceful demand.

As we stood waiting, a man wearing beat-up jeans and a tan-colored short-sleeved shirt descended the stairway on the left. He was holding a rifle, and it looked to me like he might even be a local, perhaps someone who'd broken in and was now squatting here. As he carefully edged into view, he kept the weapon trained on us, his dark eyes narrowing suspiciously.

"This is my uncle's house," I stated coldly, hoping to catch him off guard with my false bravado. "Who are you, and why are you trespassing here?"

"The man who owned this house is dead," a feminine voice suddenly rang out. "We are the caretakers of his estates, and *you* are the trespassers here."

While speaking in her heavily accented English, a woman had come down from the third floor as well, descending the stairs on the right as she studied us with bright, inquisitive eyes. Short like her companion, she wore her long, dark hair pulled back in a ponytail and was dressed in cutoff jeans paired with a white tank top. It looked like she was ready for a hot day at the beach, although the gun in her off hand, which was pointed unerringly in our direction, emphasized the seriousness of her resolve.

"Now, please," she said, "explain yourselves. And do so quickly if you do not wish to be cut down right where you stand."

3

I was unfamiliar with how my uncle had run things, except for what I'd read so far in his notes. But these places that he owned all across the world had to be cared for by someone, especially if they were on a grand scale like this mansion. The house we'd briefly visited in Tacoma had been small, more of a supply station than a real safe house, so no caretakers had been necessary. Yet it wasn't too far-fetched an idea that he'd have hirelings looking after things at some of his larger estates. Now, if there were only some way to confirm it.

"My name is Gillam," I said. "And these are my associates, Tunuhun and Jarrod. My aunt is in charge of all my late uncle's holdings, and she told us we could use these dwellings and their contents during our travels. Surely you must have some way to verify that?"

She studied Tunuhun and I closely, then glanced over at Jarrod where he stood with his hands still raised. After a few moments of silent consideration, she reached into her back pocket with her left hand, drawing forth a cell phone, and then hit the speed dial function with her thumb. Through it all she kept the gun fully trained on us, and there was no doubt in my mind she would use it if given even the slightest provocation.

"Ma'am?" she said when the call was connected. "We have someone here claiming to be your nephew. He's got a couple of other gringos with him, but they all look pretty shifty. What would you like me to do with them?"

She paused, listening to the reply, then lowered her weapon, waving it at her companion to do likewise. "I see. Yes, we will take care of it. I'll let them know. Thank you."

Tucking the phone back in her pocket, she came the rest of the way down the stairs. "Your aunt told me it's alright," she said. "You are to have full access here, and we're to assist you in any way we can. But she had to cut the conversation short in case her lines are tapped." Her suspicious eyes roved over us, noting our disheveled appearance and questionable hygiene. "You could use a bath and something to eat by the looks of it. My brother will show you to your rooms and furnish you with fresh clothing while I prepare a quick meal. Please remember not to flush any toilet paper if you have to use the facilities; Lima has lousy plumbing, and we use wastepaper baskets for the soiled tissue instead of flushing it. Trust me, you don't want to see what happens when the pipes back up around here."

With a smile tugging at the corners of her lips, she slipped the gun into her waistband and then offered me her hand. "My name is Ofelia, and this is my brother Xavier. We work for your aunt and uncle. Well, just your aunt now, ever since your uncle passed away. I am truly sorry about your loss—he was a great man."

I took the proffered hand, shaking it firmly. I was beginning to like this interesting young woman; she had a cynical attitude but still managed to find humor in the situation despite her misgivings. Her brother came down the stairs more slowly, still wary, taking his time to study us as he tucked the rifle into the crook of one arm.

"It's a pleasure to meet you," I said. "But you are correct; we're in desperate need of a shower and then some decent food. We'll gladly take you up on your offer, if that's alright?"

"Of course!" she said. "The kitchen is just down that hallway on your left. After you get washed up, just follow your nose." Turning, she gestured at Xavier. *"Apúrate y muéstrales a sus habitaciones, Bobo!"*

He frowned but then shrugged, smiling affectionately at his sister's good-natured bullying. Motioning for us to follow, he made his way back up to the third story. We climbed the stairs after him and were soon led to a series of interconnected rooms. The bathrooms were located just down the hall from our suite, so we settled into our luxurious new living quarters before heading off to the showers.

The clothing we found laid out on the beds when we returned was functional and lightweight, the type of casual attire one might expect in a tropical environment. Khaki pants and short-sleeved shirts made up the selection, and we were soon dressed and ready to head down for a midmorning repast. Fortunately, Jarrod had made it to the cargo plane with his baggage still intact. His girth would have strained the seams of my uncle's cast-off garments, so it was lucky that he'd brought his own wardrobe along. He now wore a large T-shirt over baggy pants with a multi-pocketed vest rounding out the look. With the succulent aroma of freshly prepared food guiding us, we descended the grand staircase and made our way toward the kitchen just off the main hall.

Upon entering, I could tell that this room had undergone extensive renovations. The large area now boasted top quality appliances yet retained its historic charm with a central island for food preparation and a small breakfast nook situated over by some tall bay windows. Ofelia greeted us and then ushered us all over to sit at the table, bustling about the kitchen like she knew what she was doing. My stomach made loud demands as we settled into our chairs.

Serving us with a no-nonsense flair, Ofelia dished out sausage scrambled with eggs, toasted French bread, fruit juice, and rich black coffee. Without waiting, we dug into our meal, appreciating the delicious flavors and delighting in the robust coffee, which seemed a good deal stronger than I was used to back in the States. As we ate, her brother wandered in to join us, watching us closely and then scooting his chair over to allow room for his sister to sit. Removing her apron, she tossed it onto the back of the vacant seat, settling in with a great sigh of pleasure. Then, picking up her own coffee mug, she inhaled the aroma with partially closed eyes, smiling in pure bliss.

For several minutes, there was no conversation as we concentrated on eating. But once we were well and truly sated, Ofelia raised a questioning eyebrow. "So, you are his nephew, yes?" she asked. "Tell me, what brings you here to Peru, and how can we best be of help?"

Though I'd been expecting it, the inquiry still caught me off guard. How did I even begin to explain? Would these people understand what had happened to us over the last few days? How much could I safely tell them? I decided to start at the beginning, hoping the more disturbing details could perhaps be glossed over. "We've come here seeking help in translating an artifact we found up in Alaska." Reaching into my pocket, I produced the map tile fragment, handing it over. "My uncle's tablet informs me that Dr. Huxtable would be the best person to show this to."

Ofelia studied the incised piece of stonework, eyeing the markings and then holding it up to the light so she could trace one slender finger across the symbols etched there. With an air of budding concern, she then handed it to her brother so he could take a closer look, turning back to me with a scowl that would have sent small children scurrying for cover.

"What are you not telling us?" she asked bluntly. "This artifact is clearly not something made by the hands of men. In all of my archaeological dealings, I have never before run across anything like it. As you may have already guessed, your uncle was getting into some pretty heavy shit just before his death. If we are to help you at all, we deserve to know the risks involved. And please, do not patronize me; I'm a lot smarter than I look, and I have very little patience for prevarication."

Her demeanor told me that I wouldn't be able to sugarcoat the severity of our dangerous mission. Plus, she was right; they deserved to know what they were getting into. So I spent the next few minutes bringing them up to speed on what had befallen us thus far, from the frozen Mi-Go hive in the Brooks Range to Nathrotep's interdimensional undercity, right down to the spirit of Ezra Jedidiah now inhabiting Tunuhun's body. Capping it all off, I informed them about the agents currently hot on our trail. Through it all, they both seemed more thoughtful than alarmed. It made me wonder just what my uncle had been up to that would have facilitated this calm acceptance of such a deeply disturbing tale.

"This Nathrotep you mention," she asked when I was done. "Would you say that his plans are affecting the politics in every country? How much control does he really have over the people in charge?"

"With his stranglehold on the internet and all things touched by it," I replied, "I'd say he has an overwhelming influence over the governing bodies of all nations. I didn't want to believe it at first, but if you think about what our current political situation is globally, almost every country's leadership has been in a serious downward spiral for years now. His goal at this point is to spread chaos and discord while feeding off its aftereffects. Something about the hysteria that results from civil unrest makes him stronger. And that sort of unchecked social divisiveness is happening all across the world right now."

Jarrod snorted into his coffee, then set the mug down, offended by our ignorance. "Nyarlathotep is the *embodiment* of madness! He is the messenger of the outer gods, and iffen he says he's a doin' alla them things he done told us about, then you better believe it! That bastard is a right maestro when it comes to diabolical plots and schemes. I've dealt with him afore, and we's all gonna be in a world of hurt iffen he manages to make an appearance here in the flesh."

"Nutqaqtitchuksrauruq," Tunuhun added in his quiet yet strongly worded way. And he was right; Nathrotep had to be stopped at all costs.

Ofelia's brows had drawn down during the conversation, her expression clouding over with barely contained fury as she listened to our comments. Slamming her coffee mug onto the table, she suddenly rose from her chair. *"Ese cabron!"* she exploded. "I knew there had to be someone behind it all! Well, I won't stand for it!" With that, she strode from the room, heading through the kitchen archway and leaving us all sitting there in shocked silence.

Her brother, still lazily studying the map tile fragment, glanced over at me with an amused expression coloring his dark features. "You will have to forgive my sister," he said in a richly accented voice. "She has not been herself since all of the political unrest here began. Our city, it has a population of over ten million souls. And it is divided into forty-three districts, each one with its own separate mayor. These last few years have seen a lot of conflict here in Lima, and my sister, well, she belongs to an underground movement that wishes to see the indigenous people get more rights and privileges. You can hardly blame her for being so upset—it is not every day that you find out a malignant god is controlling your leaders."

Leaning across the table, he peered curiously into Tunuhun's eyes, tilting his head to the side to get a better look. "So, do you really have an ancient, undead warlock in there with you?" he asked. "That is some seriously fucked-up shit." Glancing over at Jarrod, he continued, "And you are going to exorcise this demon from him, yes? Banish it?"

Jarrod grimaced as he considered the question. "Well, that's the plan," he grumbled. "Iffen we can ever get round to it." He was clearly still unhappy about having to wait.

Xavier whistled low under his breath, settling into his chair while draping an arm casually over the back. "From what you've just told us, it sounds like you have a lot of things to worry about right now," he said, still toying with the map tile fragment. "I could help, you know. I have connections here in Lima—know certain people in occult circles around town. And I am not unfamiliar with rituals and the necessary preparation that goes along with them.

"However," he stated, bending his arm as if making ready to toss the stone back to me, "I do not think we will have time to do any of these things." Reconsidering the fragility of the object in his hand, he instead reached out to carefully place it on the table between us. "The man you are looking for, this Dr. Huxtable? He is currently deep in the jungles at his newly discovered dig site. Another expedition is supposed to bring him supplies, but they are departing from Lima very soon— this morning, in fact. Joining them is really the only way you'll ever be able to meet with him as he's been keeping this new location a secret from everyone, even the other archaeologists he would normally confer with. It is all very hush-hush, you see."

This was indeed bad news. "Is there anyone else that you know of?" I asked. "Someone besides Huxtable who could assist us in translating this fragment?"

He considered the question, returning my inquisitive gaze with a frankness that I found somewhat disconcerting. "There is no one else who would have enough experience to help you," he finally stated. "Huxtable is the leading authority on artifacts such as this one and even dabbles in the otherworldly aspects of such things. You may find others who would look at it for you, but in order to get an accurate assessment, you will definitely need his help. What's more, it seems very familiar. I am sure that I've come across something like it before while helping Huxtable prepare artifacts for storage and later classification."

This was all new information that seemed to point us in the right direction. But in my experience, if something sounded too good to be true, it generally was. "I appreciate your offer, I really do," I told him. "But why? Why would you choose to assist us when our quest will most likely end in all our deaths? You don't even know me and have really no reason to believe me at all. For all you know, we could be escaped lunatics, judging by the tale I just told you. Why do you so readily believe us? What can you hope to gain from it?"

Leaning back again, he casually studied his hand, rubbing his thumb across his fingertips while considering the question. Finally, he gave a little sniff that briefly crinkled up his nose. "I do not think that you are mad," he stated. "I have seen things, experienced certain events, that have changed my perspective over these last few years. And working closely with your uncle and Dr. Huxtable has opened my eyes to many historical wonders, given me access to knowledge that has been lost or purposely suppressed over the centuries. I find these hidden truths to be very intriguing and wish to know more, to see more than any man has ever seen before.

"Now, my sister, she might choose to help you for reasons having to do with the treatment of our people. Perhaps try and find some way to overcome the tyranny of our oppressors and bring back the dignity and self-reliance of our once proud race. This mention of our government being manipulated seems to have really lit a fire in her belly, so I wouldn't be surprised if she decides to tag along. I, on the other hand, have various other motives."

Waving a hand in a languid arc that would seem to include the palatial kitchen in which we sat and the mansion surrounding it, he continued, "Your uncle, he was a great man. And he always took care of us, saw that we were well-fed, well-clothed, and compensated fairly for our work. But now that he is dead . . ." He let the sentence trail off, raising an eyebrow. "Let us just say that I wish to establish a *new* arrangement. A mutually beneficial arrangement. With *you.*

"The way I see it, your aunt is in control of your uncle's assets, and yet you have the ability to obtain substantial amounts of funding for your own personal use. I can make sure you find the good doctor, assist you with the exorcism, then help you defeat these Mi-Go and the deity from beyond time and space. Surely we can come to an agreement, perhaps determine just how much my aid in helping to save the world might be worth to you?"

His smile was sly and yet devoid of all malice, seemingly perpetrated by pure greed alone. And it was this simple motivation that drove him now, along with a thinly veiled interest in increasing his own growing knowledge of forbidden esoterica. As far as the reserves of wealth we had access to, the amounts were nearly limitless. But what price could truly be placed against the lives of millions? And would any amount of money we gave him now really matter if we ultimately failed? Making my decision, I returned his curious gaze with impenetrable resolve. "Name your price," I stated boldly, "and you shall have it."

His smile broadened as he offered me his hand. Taking ahold of it, we shook, sealing an agreement, for better or for worse, which could either see us defeat the evils I faced or find us all buried beneath a mountain of unstoppable madness. In my opinion, I had gotten the better end of the deal.

"What of your sister?" I asked, sipping at the remnants of my coffee. "Do you really think she might join us?"

At that exact moment, Ofelia came storming back into the kitchen, a backpack slung across one shoulder and a rifle case held in her hand. "Get your stuff together," she ordered. "You will find all the supplies you need in your uncle's weapons vault. We are leaving as soon as you are ready. If we're going to catch the plane with Dr. Huxtable's expeditionary team, then we will have to hurry." Seeing our shocked expressions, she raised her eyebrows. "Well?" she barked, "Don't just sit there! *Apurense, vamonos!*"

I glanced over at her brother, but he just smiled, shrugging and spreading his hands wide as if to say, *I told you so.*

4

Within a couple of hours, we'd found ourselves boarding a plane heading to the remote city of Iquitos. But things didn't start out so well upon our arrival at Dr. Huxtable's villa when we were first introduced to his associates. The need for secrecy about their employer's mysterious dig site was made abundantly clear, almost resulting in us being forcibly ejected from the premises. Fortunately, Ofelia helped to smooth things over by explaining we were continuing my late uncle's research. Even so, the expedition leader, a man by the name of Bryce Edwards, was still hesitant to allow us to accompany them.

At least until I showed him the map tile fragment.

After taking one look at the glyph-covered object, his attitude changed miraculously. Suddenly, we were welcomed to tag along and urged to confer with the doctor about this 'valuable find,' as he so called it. His unexpected enthusiasm did not go unnoticed, and Tunuhun eyeballed the man suspiciously afterward. But try as I might, I could obtain no further information; he simply stated that I'd have to wait and discuss it with Huxtable. Overall, I found his evasiveness off-putting, causing me to remain skeptical of his motives from that point forward.

Once we'd landed at the small airport in Iquitos, we were loaded onto a private bus heading for the port. But I soon found that traveling through this jungle-bound city could be quite unnerving. Because of its geographical location, cars were a rarity here, and instead, the roads were clogged with 'tuk-tuks.' These three-wheeled vehicles featured a covered passenger compartment and roved from one lane to the other with little regard for oncoming traffic. Upon reaching the river, I was only too happy to set foot once more on solid ground. Yet as soon as we arrived, we were whisked aboard a boat where various supplies were already being loaded. Then, after the crates were secure, we journeyed into the surrounding wetlands, traveling up the Amazon River into the lush, tropical rainforest.

Once we'd put the questionable comforts of Iquitos behind us, the other members of the expeditionary team seemed to grow increasingly tense. If I hadn't already been watching closely, I might have missed it, but they appeared to be worried about what lay ahead. The reason for their apprehension was unclear, and that made me nervous. After all, what sort of trouble were they expecting at their own dig site? At this point in our misbegotten quest, I hardly wanted to add anything to my list of things to be concerned about. In fact, I just wanted to confer with Huxtable and then continue on our way using his translations to find another Mi-Go hive. The urge to act, to somehow discover a means to stop the alien invasion before having to deal with Nathrotep and his fertile queen, was very strong. I knew that the sooner we figured things out, the quicker we could put this whole sorry mess behind us. Such were my thoughts as we sped up the river toward our mysterious destination.

The Amazon was a marvel to behold. Thick vegetation encroached upon the water to either side, yet sometimes the river grew so wide we could scarcely see the banks. Birds of all kinds were in great abundance while monkeys, sloths, and other small animals frolicked amongst the vine-covered branches. The deep, flowing waters also teemed with life, featuring innumerable varieties of fish and even some pink river dolphins following along in our wake. Late in the afternoon, Tunuhun came to join me as I stood near the prow, his expression somber and thoughtful as he leaned against the railing.

"Araqhaa napaaqtut," he said, gazing out at the passing scenery.

It was indeed quite breathtaking, the rays of the setting sun bringing the colors to life in such a way that their vibrancy seemed almost surreal. But as I lingered there savoring his steadfast companionship and enjoying the view, he suddenly stiffened. Reaching out, he grabbed my arm, drawing me away from the side of the boat and moving us further into the covered passenger area. Glancing at him curiously, I noted that his dark eyes were now scanning the rainforest with suspicious avidity.

"What is it?" I asked, dreading the answer.

"Nipaitpaitchuq," he said, pointing out the jungle's sudden, unnatural stillness.

As we edged in between the stationary deck chairs, Xavier came over to hand us both rifles, his expression grim. Grasping the firearm, I took a moment to check on the other passengers and was surprised to find them also arming themselves from open supply crates. It was an unsettling development, and I moved to confront Edwards where he stood overseeing their distribution.

"What's going on?" I asked.

"I don't know exactly," he confessed, hefting a sidearm and then jacking a round into the chamber. "But we've recently had some trouble back at the camp—something about this area has the natives all riled up. And when the jungle falls silent like this . . . well, it's a good idea to be prepared for anything. The local tribes around here can be quite aggressive, and our present course has taken us into their territory." Trying for a reassuring smile, he grasped my shoulder, giving it a squeeze. "But I wouldn't worry too much about it—it's probably nothing."

But just then, a deep, resonating ululation began, cutting him off and filling the air with the thrumming vibrations of a voice raised in a chilling, bone-shivering chant. The expression on the man's face took on a passing look of sheer terror before he got control of himself. Glancing nervously at the shoreline, he cleared his throat, his grip on my shoulder intensifying. "Make sure you keep your head down," he advised, "and I don't want to see you going anywhere near the railings for the time being, understand? I'll tell the captain to put on more speed—perhaps we can outrun them." With that cryptic remark, he was off, heading toward the wheelhouse with long, purposeful strides.

Watching him go, I was uncertain of how best to react. But Tunuhun got me moving again, grasping my elbow and then steering us both into covered positions, where we still had a clear view of our surroundings. At this point, my hunting instincts took over, and I methodically checked the rifle, making sure it was ready to fire as I scanned the passing foliage. I didn't have long to wait before our aggressors revealed themselves, emerging from the undergrowth near the river's edge.

As I watched on in stunned disbelief, I witnessed several wooden dugouts gliding forth from beneath the overhanging vegetation, paddled by determined-looking aborigines. These bow-wielding natives were small in stature, covered from head to toe in ritualistic paint and feathered adornments. And accompanying these fearsome warriors in a prominent position on the lead canoe was a terrifying figure whose own accouterments were layered in mystic symbolism. Animal skins beaded with intricate designs hung from him like a funerary shroud while a crown of jagged bones graced his head like some sort of macabre indication of his ritualistic rank. In addition to the elaborate ceremonial attire, the lower half of his brutish face was painted bright orange, with further spots of ocher-colored pigment encircling his dead-white eyes. This individual was the one chanting, and his baritone voice rose and fell in a deep, methodical intonation that inundated the air with an unclean cadence. As the other tribesmen began firing arrows, the waters around us suddenly churned with turbulent activity.

Poking my head cautiously over the top of a deck chair, I risked a glance down into the murky river, blanching in horrified shock from what I saw there.

Our boat was quickly becoming enveloped by a writhing throng of roiling tentacles. Not only that, but these thick, rubbery coils were glowing with intermittent arcs of sizzling electricity, causing sizable jolts of energy to lash out against the hull. I cried out a warning but was too late to save the captain. Seated at the wheel while furiously trying to maneuver us into deeper water, he was caught by a surge of power coming up from the keel. The cascading electrical discharge, much like a miniature lightning storm, burst from the control panel, engulfing him in a web of shock-inducing currents. With his eyes bulging from his head, he fell to the deck, his body overtaken by backbreaking seizures. And as his heels drummed the deck, there was a sputtering screech, and then, the smell of burnt ozone as the engine seized, leaving us dead in the water.

Shouting for the others to stay away from anything metal, I slid back behind cover. Yet there was complete chaos as everyone began returning fire at once from under a continuous hail of arrows. Cries of wounded men and women soon filled the air, and several people were shocked unconscious by their unfortunate proximity to the railings. As I saw someone take an arrow to the chest, falling into the depths of the river below, I decided to concentrate on my own survival. Pointing my rifle toward their shaman, I fired from almost point-blank range.

But the bullet had no effect.

It was impossible, yet my carefully aimed projectile had gone straight through him without doing the slightest bit of harm. It was as if he weren't even truly there. Without wasting any more effort on this apparently untouchable foe, I focused on the men shooting arrows instead and was relieved to see my shots pierce flesh. But after several moments of this futile exchange, Tunuhun grabbed my arm, pulling me toward the wheelhouse, where everyone else was now already headed in full retreat.

With the boat mired in a mass of electrified tentacles and our foes closing in from all sides, it seemed certain that we'd be overwhelmed. But Xavier suddenly climbed onto the roof of the cabin, removing a bandolier from around his shoulders before hurling it overboard.

"Everyone down!" he shouted, throwing himself flat.

The people around us followed suit, and Tunuhun and I could do no less. Hitting the deck, we were just in time to cover our heads as an underwater explosion heaved the boat hard over. Water and pieces of rubbery flesh rained down around us as the hull pitched in a drunken motion, sliding us back and forth between the seats. But as the rocking subsided, Xavier got to his hands and knees. "Now!" he cried. "Attack those *hijos de puta!*"

Scrambling to comply, the entire remaining complement of our beleaguered vessel took aim at the archers before their shaman could reestablish his vile chant. Several arrows still pinged off the sides of our craft, but the enemy was badly disorientated by the explosion, those left alive stunned and barely functioning. In a matter of minutes, we'd killed off a great many, sending the rest paddling back into the dense rainforest bordering the river's edge. As the boat slowly stabilized, blessed silence descended once more until we found ourselves staring at each other in bewilderment, surprised by our own survival.

Edwards had an arrow lodged in his left shoulder, but he broke it off at the shaft with a pained grimace as we gathered around him. While we stood there, bristling with weapons and still quite leery of the nearby jungle, the last light of day slowly faded, casting a pall of darkness over us all. Kneeling beside the captain's body, Edwards checked for a pulse. Then, shaking his head sadly, he closed the dead man's eyes as the remaining deckhands began lighting emergency lanterns.

"We're close to the dig site now," he stated solemnly. "We just need to figure out how to make it the rest of the way there. I don't know exactly why we were attacked, but the main camp has been experiencing similar incursions ever since we arrived." An aide with a medical kit came over as he was speaking, examining his wounds while he continued, "Everyone take stock—we need to determine our losses. Then we have to figure out how to get this boat moving again. There will be time enough to mourn after we reach the camp."

While the remaining members of the expedition team attempted to salvage what was left of the cargo, Tunuhun and I bent to study a tentacle fragment, which lay quivering nearby. From what we could see in the lantern light, it was brown in coloration with speckles of orange decorating its still twitching flesh. I was unsure of what to make of it; just what sort of river creature could have such a vast array of electrified appendages or even grow to these epic proportions for that matter?

"*Electrophorus voltai.*"

I glanced up at the softly spoken remark to find Xavier standing over us. Straightening up from my crouch, I raised an eyebrow, inviting him to elaborate.

"It is a new species of electric eel," he said. "They were discovered in this area only just recently and are capable of discharging up to 860 volts! That shaman must have been summoning them, concentrating them in a large school beneath the boat in order to disable us. Although I have never seen them grow to such a tremendous size before."

Ofelia suddenly stalked up out of the shadows, punching him solidly in the shoulder. *"Eso fue estupido!"* she hissed. "What did you think you were doing, jumping up on the roof like that? You could have gotten yourself killed!"

Rubbing his bruised deltoid, he grinned at her. "I needed to get to a higher elevation so I could throw that bandolier a safe distance away from the boat. It worked, didn't it?"

"Tonto!" she spat, poking a rigid finger into the middle of his chest. "If you *ever* do something so stupid again, I will kill you *myself!*"

Brushing aside her hand, he clasped her to his chest in a one-armed bear hug. "Don't worry, *hermanita*," he said. "That was the one stupid thing I planned on doing today—*te lo prometo!*"

"What was it that you threw in the water?" I inquired, intrigued by his resourcefulness.

"Oh, your uncle had some military-grade explosives back at the house. It was just a bandolier charge used for clearing obstacles, but I've always wanted to try one out. They work well underwater, do you not agree? Sort of like a hand grenade, but without all the shrapnel."

Behind him, I saw Jarrod pop up from amongst the cargo crates where he'd been hiding. Making his way toward us, he shook his head ponderously at the destruction revealed in the lantern light. "Them weren't no regular tribesmen," he said. "There was somethin' wrong with 'em. I could feel it!"

"And what would you know?" Ofelia demanded, rounding on him. "The indigenous people here have long suffered the ignominies of being invaded and persecuted, going all the way back to the first Spaniards who stole our land, raping and pillaging all across our beautiful country. Perhaps they were simply protecting what is rightfully theirs!"

"That may be so," he said, unperturbed by her evident wrath. "But them there fellers were definitely bespelled. No matter what they was protectin', there's some fearsome dark magic behind it!"

"Let's not bicker amongst ourselves," I said, hoping that calm rationality would prevail. "Right now, we all need to pitch in and see if we can get this boat moving again."

Fortunately, everyone agreed, and we got to work, helping to repair the damage while also struggling to determine just who we'd lost during the attack. In addition to the captain, three crew members and two of the other mission teammates were either dead or just plain missing. The boat itself had also sustained heavy damage, and because the motor was completely fried, we'd been adrift for several minutes. Edwards ordered the crew to drop anchor, tying us off so that we swung in closer to shore. It was a calculated risk but a necessary one to keep us out of the main channel.

The electrical systems were inoperable, and we'd also lost some crates overboard because of the explosion.

Luckily, we weren't taking on any water, which in and of itself was somewhat of a small miracle. We had five crew members left, with a combination of eighteen remaining archaeologists and grad students employed by Dr. Huxtable. After doing all we could to secure the boat and treat those who were wounded, we gathered again by the wheelhouse to discuss our options.

"We can't stay here," Edwards began, "but the motor is useless, and the backup engine is too small to propel us upstream with all the weight we're carrying. I propose we use the Zodiac to send a party up to the main camp. Once they reach it, they can then return with the other vessel Huxtable keeps moored there for emergencies. That way, we can get everyone to safety within a matter of hours."

"What about those people who attacked us?" one of the crew members called out. "If they return, how will we defend ourselves in the dark? We'll all be killed!"

There were grumbles of assent as everyone shifted around uncomfortably, eyeing the dense jungle growth with more than a little apprehension. "We'll set up a couple of battery-powered spotlights," Edwards replied. "Form barriers out of the remaining cargo, select people for a rotating watch. We still have plenty of firepower, and it's unlikely that they'll attack again after being so badly beaten. They'll need to regroup and gather enough reinforcements if they hope to succeed."

There was further disagreement, but in the end, we really had no other choice. A group left within the hour on the Zodiac and then returned much later with a larger ship. Attaching a towline to the bow cleat, the other vessel had us ready to go in short order, and we were soon inching our way toward the dig site. The going was slow as we fought against the current, so it took us the remainder of the night just to get there. As the rays of the morning sun crested the jungle canopy, we saw our destination ahead painted in the dawn's early light.

It was a large encampment situated in a clearing at the edge of the Amazon River. However, much of it now lay in ruins. Apparently, they'd also suffered attacks and had fortified their remaining structures accordingly. This did not bode well, but at least some of them were still alive, and with our increased numbers, we now stood a better chance of survival.

I'd been perplexed by how much firepower we were transporting, but it all made sense now that I saw what these people were up against. Having to deal with tribal warriors firing arrows, not to mention whatever dark powers their shamans possessed, would require a bolstered defensive strategy. Yet right now, all I cared about was getting this map tile fragment translated and then getting the hell out of this place—their conflict was no concern of mine, and from the look on Ofelia's face, it was something she found deeply offensive. Ideally, if we could just speak with Dr. Huxtable and then take the Zodiac back down to Iquitos, that would suit me just fine. Our mission awaited, and time was of the essence.

I only hoped that the good doctor would see it my way so we could all leave this accursed location as swiftly as possible.

5

The pier we tied up to was newly constructed and perhaps the most heavily guarded area of the compound. In the waters around it were signs of recently repelled attacks: splintered fragments of dugout canoes, along with bloated, paint-covered bodies bobbing amongst the roots of nearby trees. The smell of decaying flesh was abysmal. We were forced to cover our faces with random bits of cloth, and in some cases, our own shirt collars, just to breathe through the stench. Disembarking, we hurried away, escorted by a detachment of armed guards, who then led us through the camp.

As we left the river's vicinity, other men began unloading the damaged riverboat, assisted by the remaining crew members and a few other grad students. Glancing around, I studied the destruction caused by repeated incursions, noting the hastily erected barriers and freshly dug trenches. It looked like a war zone. The temporary structures built to house the team of archaeologists and their support staff were now in shambles, bristling with spent arrows and scorched by unclean fire.

Moving along a path created by rough-cut logs laid side by side on a muddy track, we were escorted to a command post built out of lumber and canvas. Through the open tent flap, I could see large tables covered with charts and scientific equipment, while off to one side stood a portable generator. Edwards, cradling his injured arm inside a sling, moved to the forefront of our group, in obvious pain yet eager to report to his superior. Upon entering the structure, we immediately noticed an imposingly tall man standing at the central workstation while briskly making notations on a map using a compass caliper.

He was physically fit, his loose, khaki shirt highlighting strong, sinewy arms and broad shoulders. But his reddish, salt and pepper beard and short-cropped hair made him appear more like a Roman military commander than a renowned archaeologist. While we waited for him to acknowledge our arrival, he eventually finished his calculations, then glanced up over the rims of his rectangular glasses.

After studying our disheveled appearance, he motioned to one of his aides standing nearby. "Run and fetch the doctor, won't you?" he ordered. "It appears that Bryce has taken a wound from one of those damnable arrows." Coming around the table, he twitched aside an edge of the makeshift bandage, peering down at the broken shaft with a small, disapproving frown. "We'd better have this removed straight away; we don't want it to fester. Some of those filthy jungle monkeys have been using poison-tipped arrowheads as well."

Bristling in offense, Ofelia shoved her way past me, a scowl darkening her delicate features. *"Pendejo!"* she hissed. "What do you expect them to do? You encroach upon their sacred lands, invade their ancestral temples, and profane their burial grounds. It is *you* who are the invaders here! These 'jungle monkeys', as you so call them, are the true peoples of Peru. And they are probably only protecting what is rightfully theirs!"

His intense blue eyes remained fixated on his associate's wound, ignoring her comments entirely. "Bryce," he murmured after a moment, "what in God's name were you thinking bringing strangers out to my private dig site?"

"These aren't strangers," Edwards insisted, in too much pain to be properly deferential. "This is Gillam, the nephew of the late Dr. Parsineous, and his colleagues, Jarrod and Tunuhun. You're already familiar with Ofelia and Xavier; they've helped catalog our findings back in Lima on numerous occasions. I can assure you that no one here poses any serious threat to the security of our operation."

Huxtable paused to consider that, then squared his broad shoulders, turning to face Ofelia. "You'll have to forgive my poor manners," he began. "These last few days have been . . . difficult." Clearing his throat, he continued, "That racial slur was way out of line and not the sort of thing I'm generally known for. But you have to understand that these natives came out of the jungle without warning and then proceeded to kill my people indiscriminately. I have body bags stacking up, all awaiting transport back to families who do not yet even know that their loved ones are deceased. These were students, colleagues, and in some cases, long-standing members of my personal archaeological staff. So, I hope you can ignore my momentary lack of civility—I'm afraid my frustration over our current situation has gotten the better of me." Turning back to Edwards, his face took on a pained expression. "Who else did we lose on the river last night?"

"Rodriguez and Jenny," Edwards stated, his features clouding over with grief.

Huxtable closed his eyes, lowering his head for a moment. Then, taking off his glasses, he massaged the bridge of his prominent nose, obviously overwhelmed with emotion. "Jenny's family will have to be notified along with the rest," he lamented. "Dammit! She was so young!" Shaking his head, he pulled himself together, returning his spectacles to their rightful place. "But getting back to the business at hand, you still haven't told me why these people are even here in the first place. I left explicit instructions that my exact whereabouts were to be kept under wraps until after we'd fully explored the area."

"There was no way to contact you beforehand," Edwards said, "but I had to bring them. Gillam is in possession of one of the missing relics!"

Appearing far from mollified, Ofelia stepped aside to allow me to reveal the map tile fragment in my outstretched palm. As Huxtable's eyes focused on the inscribed piece of stonework, his features paled, practically trembling with barely contained excitement.

"Everyone out," he suddenly barked, and his remaining fellow scientists scattered, fleeing through the open tent flap with unceremonious haste. Soon, it was just my companions and I standing alone with Edwards and Huxtable. Reaching out tentatively, the archaeologist paused, his eyes silently seeking my approval. With a small shrug, I allowed him to take it.

"For the love of God," he whispered, studying the artifact with awed reverence. "Wherever did you find this?"

"That isn't important right now," I said, not wanting to explain everything all over again. "Is there any way that you can translate it?"

"May I?" he asked, indicating a table filled with instruments. When I nodded my approval, he swiftly opened a rectangular container. Then, with great care, he secured the piece inside the transparent box. Sitting down at a nearby laptop, he punched in some codes, and a series of lasers played out over the fragment, scanning it from top to bottom and side to side. Within seconds, a facsimile appeared on the screen, and he studied it a moment before pulling up other similar-looking files. Using a complex algorithm, he then manipulated the images until they lined up like the pieces of some bizarre, eldritch puzzle. My tile was placed into a corner of the greater whole, and although it wasn't a precise fit, it matched up with some of the less complete sections. The entirety of it seemed incomprehensible to me, yet he was somehow able to make sense of it all.

"I've been collecting these relics for years," he said. "They appear as if carved by the same hand, yet were found in differing parts of the world." Pointing to the monitor, he continued. "As you can see here, the pieces, when aligned properly, correlate to actual locations around the globe. I've made adjustments for tectonic shifting and continental drift to get the positioning as accurate as possible." Turning back to the computer, he pulled up a map of Peru and then superimposed it on the screen. Studying the overlays, I began to see what he was referring to. The section that currently held my fragment was more complete now and seemed to fit within the geographical region surrounding the camp.

"Here's where we are, and here is the current dig site. These markings indicate that there may be something more, something even larger, hidden beyond it. And if my suppositions are correct, these new ruins may contain a treasure trove of archaeological wonders such as the world has never before seen. This could even rival Machu Picchu in terms of sheer size and splendor! Yet I've never truly been able to achieve an exact triangulation. And without more of the missing pieces, it could take decades to search so many acres of untamed wilderness. On this expedition, I'd hoped to add more pieces to my collection, but your partial fragment makes me feel as if we're on the verge of a tremendous breakthrough. So I ask again—where on earth did you find this? And perhaps, more importantly, are there any more of them?"

Studying the monitor, I ignored his question, using knowledge I'd gained from the frozen Mi-Go base to hazard an educated guess. "Can you make the cross sections semi-transparent?" I asked.

Giving me a quizzical look, he turned back to the keyboard, inputting commands until the images took on a translucence that allowed us to still see the inscriptions. "May I?" I inquired, indicating his workspace. Favoring me with a small frown, he stood, then offered me the vacant seat.

"By all means."

Sitting down, I set to work, using memories of the place Tunuhun had taken the map tile from to guide my hand. After making a few adjustments, I aligned the differing sections until they were transposed over one another like the ones I'd seen in those fantastical Mi-Go ruins. As I manipulated the projections, they began to reveal more definite details. Peering over my shoulder, Huxtable's excitement grew.

"Of course!" he exclaimed. "The tiles are designed to be viewed in overlays! Why didn't I think of that?" Staring accusingly at the monitor, he then observed, "Yet there is still something off about it . . ."

"Kalatkin nunauraq," Tunuhun offered.

"Is there a way to alter the overall color scheme?" I asked, heeding my friend's thoughtful suggestion.

Giving me a glance that simultaneously expressed both open admiration and genuine curiosity, he shooed me out of the chair, then quickly sat down, inputting more lines of code. "What color did you have in mind?"

"I would start with different shades of orange."

Getting back to work, he punched in another set of commands, and we all watched as the images changed once more, traveling through variations of color until the picture snapped into greater focus. Yet even then, I could tell there was still something missing. "Do you have any way to pull this up three-dimensionally?"

Making some minor adjustments, he imported the stacked files into another folder, then powered up a flat, black instrument sitting next to the laptop. Within a few moments, the layers we'd been studying appeared in a holographic image, hovering just above the surface of this unfamiliar device. I must admit that I was duly impressed.

"New technology from China," he stated, seeing my unfeigned interest. "They can do the most amazing things with computer imaging these days. I find that it comes in quite handy for topography and even some forms of underground geological mapping."

We all stared at the hologram, but it was obvious that the segments still did not align properly. The missing pieces—and our unfamiliarity with the original design itself—were perhaps playing a part in denying us a clearer view. For some reason, the smaller sections in the middle expanded outward, forming irregular, almost cone-shaped variances.

Upon further consideration, I realized we were going about this entirely the wrong way. We were trying to study the problem using human perceptions when what we needed to do was see it from a Mi-Go's point of view. The hive we'd found had been filled with certain shapes, laid out in patterns that repeated themselves over and over.

"Can you invert these and then apply geometrics?" I asked.

"Of course," Huxtable answered. "Were you thinking of any particular shape?"

"Try hexagons."

The doctor's fingers flew over the keys, and the construct wavered as it went through a series of evolutions. As the smaller sections moved to the outer edges and the larger pieces were placed in the middle, a more coherent visual formed. As I watched on, captivated by the ongoing process, the layers solidified into a definite shape, becoming more clearly delineated. It was still missing vast amounts of data, and those areas were blank, but within the parameters we'd forced upon it, the map revealed itself in all its three-dimensional glory.

What now appeared floating above the imaging device was a combination of interlocking hexagons, almost like a multilayered dodecahedron. Using a globe of the world as a comparison, Huxtable was able to pinpoint our exact location. Beyond that, this complex alien atlas showed us a much larger area marked by indecipherable symbols.

It had to be another one of the ancient Mi-Go outposts.

"We'll need to leave immediately," Huxtable declared, rising from the chair. "It could take us all day to get there, and we must reach it before nightfall."

"Who do we have currently guarding the dig site?" Edwards asked.

"Lenny and his team," Huxtable replied sourly. "Not my first choice, but they seem to enjoy this type of dangerous assignment and were already spoiling for a fight after last night's raid. Two of our interns were killed during the attack, and I believe Lenny was romantically involved with one of them. He's formed some sort of personal vendetta because of it. We can gather them up as we pass by there if needed."

Xavier had wandered over to the display and now stood staring down at the interlocking shapes, his emotions unreadable as he spoke to the doctor. "What about that hostile tribe?" he asked. "If they have been giving you trouble, even to the point of trying to stop us from reaching the outpost last night, what is to keep them from attacking us again along the way? There must be something we can do to gain safe passage through their lands."

With a pained expression, Huxtable reluctantly returned the Peruvian's curious gaze. "We originally had a brace of guides," he stated quietly. "They went out one night to speak with the natives after discovering them lurking about the camp. But they never returned. The next morning . . ." Swallowing heavily, he was clearly reluctant to go on, but then bravely mastered himself. "In the morning, we found what remained of them—it wasn't pretty." Shaking off the dark recollections, he continued, "I'm afraid these aborigines don't act like any we've ever encountered before. They only come out at night, and all our efforts to determine their whereabouts during the day have thus far met with complete failure. It's as if they simply melt back into the jungle before daybreak. Their behavior is most unsettling."

Xavier considered this briefly. "My people are children of the sun and earth," he finally offered, "so these nighttime raids are definitely abnormal. And our shamans do not usually practice the dark arts—it is not our way."

"Them there shamans, or whatever the hell they was, reeked of pure evil," Jarrod added. "And them spells they was a castin' had nothin' to do with true shamanism! Iffen that's what we're up against, it'll take a lot more than guns and bravado to get past 'em."

"Jarrod is somewhat of an expert in matters of the occult," I explained, seeing Huxtable's eyebrow raised in curiosity.

"And what's more, he is right," Xavier added. "While there are still some who use black magic in certain circles, it is mostly reviled here. Our beliefs stem from a deep respect for the environment, and our spiritual leaders tend to commune peacefully with the world around them instead of trying to go against the very fabric of reality itself. So, these people, whoever they were, must have had some ulterior motive for these unprecedented supernatural attacks."

"But what if they're just another isolated tribe?" Ofelia said. "There are still a few who shun all contact with the outside world. They could merely be defending their own territory, attempting to stop the pilfering of their sacred grounds. Maybe we should try to communicate with them again."

"As I indicated earlier, we've already tried that," Huxtable blustered. "In fact, we've done everything short of abandoning the dig site itself! And the area we're exploring is a series of moldering ruins overgrown with dense tropical jungle. There is absolutely no indication that they've been used for anything else in ages. All the tribes we've previously encountered have utilized their ancestral temples, made offerings, featured them in rituals and other important events. Yet that is simply not the case here. In fact, these people just randomly appeared out of the depths of the jungle one night and then attacked without warning. Furthermore, in all my research before beginning our current excursion, I found no evidence of anyone living in this remote area. One can only surmise that these people are not just another run-of-the-mill previously undiscovered tribe."

While this debate was informative, it was getting us nowhere. I needed to refocus our energies on the expedition itself. The sooner we found what we were looking for, the quicker we could figure out a way to use it against the pending Mi-Go invasion and perhaps even Nathrotep himself.

Yet it was hardly fair to bring the others into such a potentially dangerous situation without giving them forewarning. What Tunuhun and I had discovered in the mountains of the Brooks Range was a hive of sentient insectoids belonging to an advanced alien race. They could now be considered a known threat, and it was even possible we'd come into contact with them again sometime. But another confrontation here in Peru seemed highly unlikely. The previous base had been frozen in time, its inhabitants caught in a hibernation cycle. This newly pinpointed area was most likely just an ancient rotting tomb filled with potentially useful technology, but otherwise long abandoned. At least that's what I was hoping. Having another run-in with a swarm like the one we'd stumbled across a few days ago was not something I'd care to ever experience again.

As I opened my mouth to point out the potential dangers we could be facing, I was interrupted by a commotion outside the tent. It was the distant murmur of angry voices growing louder by the minute. With a final explosion of expletive-filled lunacy, a man burst past the guards, shoving his way into the tent with his torn clothing covered in blood.

"Dr. Huxtable!" he cried, staggering forward. "The dig site has been overrun!"

6

The man had clearly been pushed far beyond the limits of his own endurance. In fact, by the time the medical staff arrived to treat his wounds and extract the arrowhead from Bryce's shoulder, he seemed about ready to keel over. With all the missing strips of peeled-away skin leaving behind a gruesome trail of oozing lacerations, his features were truly horrific to behold. And from where I was standing, the raw singe marks covering his stubbled chin were also clearly visible. As the medics cleaned him up and began dressing his wounds, he twitched and shuddered spasmodically, sweat pouring off him from more than just the tropical heat.

Meanwhile, Huxtable's pained expression had become overshadowed by genuine remorse. After waiting for the man to be patched up, he tentatively stepped forward, eyeing his bandaged colleague with a look of undeniable concern.

"Lenny," he said gently, attempting to catch the man's attention, "are you able to tell us what happened?"

The man started, glancing around in confusion. Then, snatching a water bottle from one of the medics, he drained it before slumping forward again, resting his elbows across trembling knees. For a moment, he just sat there, face twitching like a palsied old man as he attempted to gather his scattered thoughts. When he was finally able to focus on Huxtable, his bloodshot eyes were wild, almost feral.

"They're dead," he stated, chewing over the words before spitting them out. "All of 'em: Jake, Thomas, even little Petey—every last one of 'em!" Rubbing a shaking hand across his eyes, he took in a deep, steadying breath, then shook his head vigorously as if to clear away the painful memories. As he pulled himself together, righteous indignation began to eclipse his overwhelming fear. "We gotta kill 'em, Doc. Wipe 'em all out! If Bryce is here, that means we got the munitions you ordered, right? Well, let's put 'em to good use. If we leave now, we can take 'em by surprise, ambush them sonsofbitches before they even know what hit 'em!"

"But what happened exactly?" Huxtable pressed. "If you can recount the details of the attack, perhaps then we can all get a better idea of what we're up against. Was it more of the same? Archers concealed in the trees, methodical chanting, strange lights in the depths of the forest?"

Lenny's features crumpled as he fought against reliving the hell he'd just been through. Clasping his shaking hands tightly around the empty water bottle, he swallowed heavily, groping for words. "It weren't like them other times, no," he managed. "We had things all set this time around, had a real plan. Petey and me, we learned some jungle tactics a while back. We knew how to fight in this type of terrain, so's we set about making it real hard for 'em. Rigged us up some trip lines, snares, even a few covered pits. Them temple steps with all that rubble strewn about? That was where we made our stand, with plenty of bonfires lit in a big circle to expose any of them bastards what chose to rush us. We had it all worked out in advance, gave them only set paths leading to the killing grounds. We figured it was gonna be like shooting fish in a barrel. But we were wrong . . ."

Muscle spasms set his chin quivering again, then migrated upward, causing his right eyelid to flutter involuntarily. With a concentrated effort, he haltingly continued, "There weren't no arrows this time—no strange lights—none of that stuff like before. Instead . . . instead it was just all that damn *clicking*." He paused, working up the courage to go on. "That noise, it was quiet at first but then grew louder, like it were coming from all around us. There was something out there, something that none of us had ever even heard before. And it was stalking us, playing with us. Petey shot up a flare, but we still couldn't see a goddamn thing! Nothing but close-packed trees and brush. Then the clicking got closer. We . . . we didn't know what to do—there just weren't nothing to shoot at, and none of our traps was working like they were supposed to. And that fuckin' sound! It was coming from everywhere. It backed us up right against them stone doors looking for something we could fight, anything we could blast away at. But there just weren't nothing there, nothing at all . . .

"That's when they got Petey. Something just snaked down from above us and snatched him right off the steps! I tried to help, grabbed his legs, started shooting up at whatever it was that had him. But it weren't no use! Whatever it was just dragged him away, kicking and screaming. We couldn't see 'em, couldn't fight 'em. So's we ran. Ran into the jungle heading back this way, trying to reach safety. But them damn things just kept snatching people left and right as we fled! We couldn't see much— just long, slimy arms lashing out from beneath bushes and trees as we ran past. It took me the rest of the night just to make it back here. I guess I was the lucky one . . ."

"But your wounds," Huxtable observed. "If you didn't directly contend with any opponents, then how did you sustain these terrible injuries?"

The man paused, glancing up at the doctor, then back down at himself, realizing perhaps for the first time that he was sorely wounded. "I . . . I don't know," he admitted in a small, bewildered voice.

"Well, that tears it," Huxtable announced. "We're getting the hell out of here. I will not risk any more of my people going up against something that we know next to nothing about. Bryce, load up the boats and see that repairs are made. I don't care if you have to rig up a secondary motor on the back of that damaged vessel, just see that it gets done!"

A crowd had formed outside the command post as word spread throughout the camp of Lenny's return. As we readied ourselves to depart, frustration threatened to overwhelm me. We were so close! Yet how could we make it to this previously undiscovered location all on our own if the jungles were filled with hostile creatures? As I considered our options, several people forced their way through the tent flap, led by a man with smoldering eyes and bleach-blond hair. Upon seeing him enter, Lenny straightened up, almost coming to attention while wiping at his filthy, torn clothing in mortified embarrassment. The larger man immediately knelt down next to him, placing a huge, calloused hand on his shoulder.

"Are you alright?" he inquired. "I heard what happened. Don't worry—we're gonna get those bastards!"

Rising back to his feet, the newcomer glared daggers at Huxtable. "What kind of a two-bit operation are you running here?" he demanded. "We have missing personnel, but I hear that you're already talking about leaving! What we need to do is organize a search party and then get after whoever did this. The trail grows colder the longer we wait."

Huxtable clearly did not appreciate this challenge to his authority. "Those missing men are most likely dead," he finally stated, regret coloring his tone, "and I cannot, in all good conscience, order anyone else to risk their lives on such a fool's errand. The search will have to wait until we can gather a force large enough to overcome whatever's out there. Since we currently don't know what we're really up against, venturing forth again now would be far too dangerous."

"You may be in charge of the expedition," the man snarled, "but a good chunk of the funding came from my family's generous donations! I will not leave here without the rest of my team. They could still be alive, could be out there right now just waiting for rescue. Since we're newly supplied, we now have enough firepower to take back what is rightfully ours. We can drive away any opposition we find long enough to recover our missing people and secure my investment while we're at it. And I don't need your permission to do that; my men answer to me, not you!"

Huxtable's expression darkened like a thundercloud as he waved an open hand toward his associate. "This is Jon Noe," he said by way of belated introduction, "my head of security and the leader of what's left of my ground support." Then, closing the distance between himself and the security chief, he stared the larger man down. "You may be in charge of your own team, but none of them could possibly be stupid enough to want to go back out there after what's just happened. I say we leave here immediately and then regroup in Iquitos. We need to find more men to bolster our ranks, not go running off into the jungle on some wild goose chase. It's the most sensible thing to do under the circumstances, and you know it!"

Jon glanced around, eyeballing me and my comrades as he took notice of us for the first time. "Who the hell are these people anyway?" he demanded. "Why are they even here if you didn't intend to press forward? I say we put it to a vote. Everybody's already gathered together outside now anyway. Let's just see who's willing to fight and who wants to run away like a bunch of fucking chickenshits. I think you'll find that most of us aren't as easily intimidated as you apparently are. What are a few aborigines against all of our superior firepower and military training? We're resupplied and prepared for a counter strike—I say that we take advantage of the opportunity!"

"The opportunity for what?" Huxtable exploded. "Charging blindly into certain death? You're asking me to put everyone here at risk. Well, I won't do it! It's no longer just simple tribesmen we're facing; there's something else out there now, something we cannot possibly handle without more able-bodied men. And with all of your military background and expertise, surely even you can see that this is a trap? To go after whatever's stalking us right now would be suicide!"

"Whatever's waiting for us, it won't be ready for the world of hurt that I intend to unleash," Jon stated confidently. "My men and I have been through worse situations than this. These *charapa* may have taken us by surprise a couple of times, but now we're more than ready for them. Besides, we've already unloaded the second boat and distributed all the arms and equipment. If whatever attacked Lenny wants to tangle with us again, then it's their funeral . . ."

"I do not think that you fully comprehend the dangers you will be facing," Xavier quietly interjected.

We all turned to find him intently studying the three-dimensional map. Seemingly mesmerized by its geometric layers, he continued, "I grew up around here. For a few years, I even worked as a guide for one of the wilderness lodges. So I know how to navigate the deeper jungles, know what sort of obstacles we would face even without the threat of unknown assailants."

Tuning toward the security chief, he met Jon's cold, hard stare unflinchingly. "There are many ways to die in the Amazon. A lot of it is covered in bogs and swamps, with small waterways running throughout. Being this close to the river, you would need flat-bottomed canoes to traverse those places safely. Otherwise, you would become trapped, cut off by tributaries, or sucked into clinging, mud-filled sinkholes. The jungle here is very unforgiving, and within its labyrinth of closely packed vegetation, it would be very easy for you to become irretrievably lost. In short, you will need my help if you are to succeed."

"And just who the fuck are you?" Jon snapped.

Taking a menacing step forward, Ofelia poked a rigid forefinger directly into the man's broad chest. "You better watch your tongue, you inbred ape!" she hissed. "Unless you are wanting a mouth full of broken teeth!"

Laying a restraining hand on her arm, Xavier grinned in appreciation of her moxie. "My name is Xavier Alvarez Cordova, and this is my sister, Ofelia," he stated. "And you should listen to me if you want to survive." Turning to Huxtable, he indicated the overlay which hovered behind the Mi-Go dodecahedron. "Exactly how accurate is this?" he asked.

"That image was taken from the most recent satellite photos and then expanded upon by my own exploratory research," Huxtable said. "We waited for the dry season in order to begin our excavation here due to fluctuating water levels. So this is as up to date as I could make it, given the transformative nature of the immediate area."

Xavier studied the map again, comparing it to the alien atlas before jabbing a finger toward several key points on its surface. "If I am not mistaken, this is where the attacks are occurring, around the base camp, and also here, at this section of the river where our boat was damaged, yes? And over here is where we need to be, correct? Judging by the topography, the region on the other side of our destination is at a higher elevation, perhaps indicating a small rise or some sort of gradual foothills leading up to those mountains beyond it."

"Yes, that's right," Huxtable agreed.

"How many canoes do you currently have on hand?" Xavier asked.

"Quite a few—we use them mostly for mapping out the surrounding waterways."

Xavier indicated the Amazon River's proximity on the map. "We are still a ways from the main channel, but if we were to go back out and then follow the river around to this point here," his finger traced a line to a location beyond the undiscovered site, "then we should be able to take the smaller canoes and make our way toward the foothills on the other side. As you can see, the Amazon doubles back, and utilizing this route would not only be more efficient, but it would also place us closer to our intended target. Plus, we would completely avoid any potential enemies still lurking around the dig site."

Jon took note of what Xavier was saying, closely inspecting the map. "How does that help us right now?" he asked. "I want to find my missing men before wiping those bastards out, not completely avoid them."

"Well, I am not a military man," Xavier said, gazing up at the security chief. "But having control of the high ground is a well-known advantage, is it not? Once there, we can then lure the natives toward us or simply outflank them by having extra men sweep the jungles, starting from here. Huxtable has already stated that you have been unable to locate their hidden refuge during the day. Between here and this new location is the most likely place that you will find it. Besides, judging from the story that Lenny has just told us, your men are probably already dead. These natives seem to be attacking you in an attempt to drive you all away or simply kill you outright. So, it is doubtful that you will find those missing men of yours still alive, especially if there is something else out there, something far more dangerous than just painted warriors with poison-tipped arrows."

Ofelia was clearly appalled. "So you are going to help these gringos kill our own people now?" she exclaimed, grabbing his arm. "*Hermano*, please! Reconsider what you are saying!"

Ignoring her, Xavier kept his attention focused solely on the security chief as Jon considered his proposition. Rubbing his chin thoughtfully, the larger man finally glanced down at the Peruvian, a look of dubious admiration crossing his blocky features. "I like it," he announced. "You may not have a military background, but you sure as hell understand the basics of winning a fight. Let's go and see if anyone else agrees with us, shall we?"

In the end, a vote was taken, and we wound up with fifty extra men while the doctor and his remaining staff would go with the other boat back to Iquitos. The plan was for them to pick up more hired hands and then head back to the base camp to await further instructions. Huxtable had been indecisive at first because he just couldn't bear the thought of someone else making a discovery that he'd been after for years. But he then decided that the safety of his team was more important before helping Jarrod and I secure the occult book and my uncle's electronic journal inside waterproof belt pouches. Once everyone was ready, we loaded the canoes onto the larger boat and then took it out to the main channel before following it around to the closest point beyond the undiscovered ruins.

The shoreline was situated quite a ways back from the main river, so we had to take the canoes through a series of densely overhung waterways to reach it. Once the early morning rain had cleared away, the day soon became uncomfortably hot. But the sunlight filtering down through the leaves caused bursts of intermittent illumination, making for an astoundingly beautiful backdrop of multihued scenery as we progressed through the tangled mangroves.

Living within the trees were many small animals and insects, and I soon became quite enamored by the charms of the local ecosystem. To be honest, it was a far cry from what I was used to back in northwest Alaska. Tunuhun seemed equally captivated as well, spending much of his time studying our surroundings with an uncharacteristic expression of childlike wonder.

After a while, the geography changed, and we found ourselves coming up out of the marshlands. Xavier secured our landing on a muddy bank angling up from the water, and after disembarking, we organized our supplies and took stock of our surroundings. It was still midmorning when he left to scout ahead, seeking to find us the safest possible route. With nothing left to do, my companions and I joined the rest of the men as they sat checking their weapons and preparing for the impending hike through unknown territory.

When Xavier returned, the day was leaning toward late afternoon, and the rest of us were eager to begin our trek. Leading the way, he took us along paths marked out during his earlier foray. The trees here were immense, adorned with crisscrossing vines and a stunning variety of other indigenous plant life. It was as if we were walking through an ancient, primordial forest. Ferns and brushy vegetation grew thick along the ground here as well, forcing us to use machetes to hack our way past several increasingly troublesome spots.

Sweat was soon pouring off everyone as we forged ahead. We'd put on plenty of bug spray that morning, yet the insects here were somehow immune, so we were constantly swarmed by clouds of blood-sucking pests. It was an uncomfortable excursion, although one of such beauty and rare natural splendor that I was hard-pressed to find fault with it.

Under any other circumstances, I knew I would have been immeasurably fascinated by our surroundings, enjoying the tropical habitat to its fullest extent. But now, heading as we were toward unknown danger, I was instead filled with a tremendous amount of anxiety. I was hoping we'd reach our destination without further incident but kept agonizing over thoughts of being attacked at any moment. The feeling was disquieting, to say the least. As we made our way through the uncharted wilderness, the constant worry did nothing to steady my already tenuous resolve.

It wasn't until the sun began dipping toward the far horizon that we reached a rocky expanse situated at the base of some low-lying hills. It was here that Xavier had been leading us, and he announced we'd set up camp there for the night, further informing us that we'd continue our journey in the morning. Gazing at the great swath of undulating treetops as they rolled away across the hills and into the clouds above us, I was daunted by the prospect of an extended climb. Yet there was no use in worrying about it now, so I pitched in with the rest to set up tents and prepare field rations over a small fire. In short order, we'd settled in, ready to wait out the coming darkness with sentries guarding the camp on a rotational basis. As I was eating beef stroganoff out of a freeze-dried meal pouch, Tunuhun came over and sat down beside me. Catching my attention, he then jerked his chin toward the far side of the clearing.

Following his steely gaze, I noticed Ofelia standing at the edge of the jungle on the other side of the camp. She was studying the men as they prepared to bed down, and once she was certain no one was watching, she slipped away into the shadowy undergrowth. I was about to go investigate this unusual behavior when Xavier walked over with a lazy grin spread across his sparsely bearded features.

"I have something of great interest to show you," he said. "Follow me if you want to see a thing that is truly astounding."

Rising to our feet, we invited Jarrod to join us as we followed Xavier back down the trail. After a few dozen meters, he split off to one side through some heavier brush. And once we'd breached this living barrier of leaves and tangled branches, we found ourselves in a sort of bowl-shaped depression enclosed by rocky outcroppings on three sides. It didn't seem natural, and my suspicions were confirmed when Xavier pulled aside some vines that covered the back wall. His actions revealed the mouth of a cave surrounded by ancient inscriptions. The unveiling of this hidden aperture took us all by surprise, and we gathered close to marvel at its wonders.

The level of detail put into the carvings was a testament to the skill of the ancient artist. It was all imagery done in the typical Peruvian style, with curving lines and deftly chiseled strokes delineating figures in bold relief. Here were stylized animals and representations of people depicted in ritualistic poses, an interwoven band of exquisite etchings that would have been the dream discovery of any archaeologist who stumbled across them. Intermixed throughout the design was a serpent encapsulating the entire motif. I did not know where this man-made entrance led, nor even what the carvings signified, but they seemed to have some deeply personal meaning to Xavier.

"These ruins are incredible," I said, "but we're losing the light. Couldn't this have waited until morning?"

"I thought it would be best to show it to you now," he replied, "before those lumbering idiots back at the camp got wind of it."

Puzzling over his odd statement, I took a closer look, hoping to fathom what he was getting at. Then, with a small shrug, I gave up in perplexity. "I'm not sure I fully understand the importance of your discovery. Please enlighten us."

He nodded, turning to trace a finger along the markings, indicating certain details as he explained. "My people have a rich spiritual history going back many thousands of years. Here you can see representations of the condor, the puma, and the snake. These animals are sacred to my people and represent certain aspects of the gods. But if you look even closer, I think that you will notice something else, something entirely unique."

Leaning forward, I peered at the carvings again in the diminishing light. As my eyes roved along the fantastical designs, certain aspects began to make themselves known to me. Woven throughout the intricate carving was a distinct pattern done in a differing aesthetic, and my pulse accelerated as it dawned on me what these additional markings signified.

They exactly matched the ones found on the map tile fragment I still carried in my pocket. And I could suddenly see that the lines and indentations from the Mi-Go script flowed throughout the entire band of artwork, mysteriously adding to the imagery encircling the entrance of this ancient jungle ruin.

As he saw understanding blossom across my once doubtful features, he grinned, nodding in approval. "These carvings are very old," he said. "And the fact that Mi-Go pictographs have been incorporated into them indicates that the tribes who once lived here must have had something to do with those aliens. Given more time, we could study this, perhaps unravel the mystery behind it." Pointing to the snake, which slithered throughout the entire piece, he continued, "The snake represents the infinite, a new life we ascend to after death, another realm entirely. For us, this has no negative connotation like in your Christian beliefs, but instead, indicates rebirth into another plane of existence. To be associated with the symbols you say are from a race of interstellar beings means that my ancestors once had contact with them, may have even traveled the stars. Having the snake in this carving could very well link the histories and beliefs of my people with that of the Mi-Go themselves."

His excitement was infectious. But if what he was saying were true, then why hadn't our planet been taken over eons ago? If these carvings were indeed only a few thousand years old, then didn't it prove that the Mi-Go were still here at that time, may have even influenced the entire Incan civilization? My mind whirled with the implications. But as I stood in stupefied wonder, Jarrod leaned past me, studying the images in the failing light.

"That there ain't no snake," he stated bluntly.

Xavier's face clouded over in consternation, staring at the portly man in apparent disbelief. Then, taking out a flashlight, he turned back to the mouth of the cave, playing the light over the engravings to get a better look. "What do you mean?" he demanded, "this is clearly . . ."

A sudden eruption of gunfire and blood-curdling screams interrupted him, and we swiftly hunkered down against the nearby rock wall, sliding into a protective huddle. The cacophony of a battle being waged close by indicated a massive struggle was now ensuing back where we'd left the others. In that moment, I could only assume that our attempts at circumventing the danger had failed. It would appear that whoever had previously been stalking the archaeological expedition had somehow managed to catch up with us once more.

7

The ongoing battle sounded horrendous, the screams of the dying mixing with the staccato bursts of automatic weapons fire to create a cacophony of chaos that was heart-wrenching to hear. Grabbing the vines hanging from the incline above us, Xavier and I clambered up the slope, leaving the less-than-agile Jarrod behind to guard our retreat. Upon reaching the top, we crawled through the verdant undergrowth, then parted the leafy branches to get a better view.

Within the falling twilight, the clearing before us was a writhing mass of rampaging combatants. Painted bodies sprang from the shadows, leaping upon the heavily armed soldiers, their ululating battle cries shrill and defiant as they plunged spear and hatchet into soft, exposed flesh. But Jon had rallied his men, and they now fought with an unmatched ferocity, their weapons felling foes by the dozens. Yet even so, their adversaries seemed endless. Someone shot up a flare, and within the amber-painted maelstrom churning below it, I saw not only the inevitable end of our ill-fated expedition but also the impending death of the whole human race.

The jungle savages were indefatigable as they fought beneath the flare's glowing light, and I had to wonder; was it madness that drove them? Or were they simply defending some kind of sacred ground upon which we'd unwittingly tread? I did not know the reasoning behind the attack, but as I watched on, they swiftly encircled the small band of soldiers left alive. And as Jon and his men struggled valiantly against such overwhelming odds, they were forced to give ground until they stood back to back at the very center of the clearing.

"Alla, amii," Tunuhun pointed out, watching from where he lay concealed next to me.

He was right; these people seemed different from the ones who'd attacked last night. Perhaps even an entirely separate tribe. As I pondered over the possible significance of this observation, Xavier jumped to his feet.

Grabbing his forearm, I yanked him back down. "Are you insane?" I hissed.

"I have to find Ofelia!" he cried, eyes wild in the flare's fading light.

"She's not caught out in the middle of all that—we saw her sneaking away into the forest just before you came to show us the overgrown ruins."

Some of the fight went out of him as my words sank in. "If it is as you say, then she may yet still be alive, could have had a chance to hide before the attack. Which way did she go? I have to find her and then lead her back here to safety."

"If you break cover, you're as good as dead," I stated flatly. "Our only hope now is to retreat to that cave.

From there, we can at least try and figure out how best to survive the oncoming night. If we're still alive in the morning, then we can go look for her."

He wasn't happy hearing my advice but saw the wisdom in it. Backing away, we retraced our path, then shimmied down the vines to land in a crouch next to the overgrown entrance. But Jarrod was no longer there. Glancing around, I felt cold, hard fear blossom within me, constricting my chest as it pulsed through my veins. Where could he have gone? Had he been discovered while awaiting our return? Without him, we were doomed; he had possession of Charmides Treatise on Mystical Maleficence and was also the only one who could use it to banish Ezra from Tunuhun's body. Searching the ground, I looked for any sign of his whereabouts, seeking footprints or traces of blood that might indicate what had happened. As I continued scanning for clues, an unexpected series of rustling movements came from inside the cave itself.

With an eerie slowness, the vines covering the ruins parted to either side, and then both Jarrod and Ofelia were suddenly peeking out at us. When they urgently beckoned us forward into the cavern's ominous mouth, we scrambled to comply, letting the leaves and branches fall back into place behind us.

Grabbing Ofelia by the shoulders, Xavier shook her gently, trying to appear stern even as a silly grin was spreading across his swarthy features. "Where have you been?" he cried. "I was worried sick that you had somehow gone and gotten yourself killed!"

Her crooked smile was slightly mocking. "I had to go potty," she stated simply. "The last thing I wanted was a bunch of *pendejos* watching me, so I went out into the jungle to find a more private spot to do my business. When the attack started, I hid until I could make my way toward the river. That was when I found this gringo standing here all by himself, and he filled me in on the rest. We decided it would be safer to wait inside than to risk joining you at the top of the ridge."

Choking back a laugh that was half a sob, Xavier gathered her into his arms, hugging her tightly. "Well, don't ever do that again, *entiendes*?" he whispered into her hair. "You just about gave me heart failure!"

"What, you want I should tell you when I have to go pee from now on?" She shoved at him playfully. "You wanna hold my hand while I tinkle?"

Their reunion was touching, but right now, we had more immediate concerns. Closing the scant distance between us, I laid a hand on Xavier's shoulder. "We're all glad that she's okay," I said. "But we should get out of here as soon as possible. There's no telling how quickly those natives will be able to track us down. Do you have any suggestions?"

While he considered the question, the ongoing sounds of battle could still be heard in the distance, gunfire and screams filling the night air with undiminished fury. There had to be some way to survive this, some path that skirted the edges of the camp and then led up to the Mi-Go ruins beyond it. The odds were stacked against us, but I held firm to the belief that we would still somehow prevail.

Thus emboldened by my unwavering resolve, I signaled to Tunuhun, and he crept to the entrance, parting the overgrowth carefully before peering out into the darkening jungle. I trusted him to be my eyes and ears, placing my life in his capable hands as I'd done so many times before. Then, turning back to Ofelia, I attempted to gather more intel. "Did you see which direction the natives came from? It seems to me that they should have had this whole area surrounded by now. Yet you somehow made it past them unscathed. How did you manage it?"

"I think they must have come down from the hills," she replied. "It looked to me like they slipped through the trees from above and then spread out before attacking. But I'm not sure why they struck our camp before encircling it."

"What happened to our sentries?" I pondered. "We should have at least had some sort of advanced warning."

"Not necessarily," Xavier said. "These people are closely in tune with the jungle here. They could easily have snuck up on us without raising the alarm. In fact, given what my sister has just told us, I am reasonably sure they are out there even now, just waiting for us to exit this cave. Why they have not yet come in after us, I do not know. But they *are* out there—of that you can be certain."

"Then how did Ofelia get past them?"

Nostrils flaring in indignation, she glared at me. "You forget that I grew up around here too," she spat. "And I am fully capable of taking care of myself, thank you very much! Once I sensed them around me, I chose to remain unseen. They were so focused on the camp that they did not expect someone small like me to be squatting in the bushes. After they swept past, it was too late to warn anyone, so I chose to head for the river. I figured it would be what Xavier would do next if he somehow managed to survive."

Her explanation seemed plausible, but something still didn't feel right. As I stood silently analyzing everything she'd said, Tunuhun suddenly made the hand signal for danger. Joining him, I peered out between the parted vines and branches.

At first, I couldn't see much of anything, but the more I studied our surroundings, the more I began to perceive details that anyone else might have missed. Growing up as a subsistence hunter in Alaska had ingrained in me the need to be perpetually observant, to be able to track prey through various types of terrain. And although this was a different kind of forest than what I was used to, the principles I'd learned still applied.

Sliding in next to me, Xavier gazed into the darkening gloom, then sighed. "Sometimes I hate being right," he stated glumly.

In the purplish twilight, the local flora had taken on the darker hues of a nocturnal environment. Long shadows grew steadily as the light faded from the heavens, painting the vibrant scenery in layers of crisscrossing contrast. It was beautiful in its own way, the canopy overhead swaying gently in the breeze while the trees themselves, tall as the ancient sentinels of a bygone age, towered above. Insects, lizards, and birds flitted through the foliage in search of a meal or perhaps heading off to roost for the evening. But also concealed within this wondrous profusion of lush greenery were the people who lived there.

It was hard to make them out due to their painted bodies blending in with the surrounding vegetation, but my earlier observations appeared to be correct. They were definitely not the same tribe that had attacked us before. The natives from last night's raid on the river had been painted in grays and oranges, their faces accentuated with spots of yellow and ocher. But these fearsome warriors were decorated in more muted pigments. Splashes of green and brown held sway, with darker streaks of umber and black creating more muted bands of color that aided in their stealthy camouflage. Some wore skirts of woven grass while others simply sported loincloths and a profusion of feathers festooning their shaggy, unkempt hair. If they hadn't been standing at the very edges of the tree line, I might not have even seen them at all. Yet they did have one thing in common with our previous foes: the intense predatory stares of carnivorous animals as they stood silently watching.

I signaled to Tunuhun, and he let the vines fall back into place, once more concealing the entrance to our dubious refuge. There was no doubt in my mind that they knew we were in here; why they hadn't already attacked was the real mystery. Mulling it over, I turned to Xavier, seeking the information I'd need in order to plot a viable course of action.

"They're definitely out there," I said. "But why are we still alive? They must know that there's no way we can resist them."

"They's afeared," Jarrod murmured, his voice quavering.

We all turned at his comment, but his presence was now only a darker spot of blackness standing behind us. I didn't know why he suddenly believed that, but his unconventional wisdom had proven trustworthy in the past. So I reached out, groping forward to lay my hand reassuringly on his trembling forearm.

"What exactly do you mean . . ." I began.

"I believe that he is right," Xavier interjected. "For some reason, they do not want to come near these ruins. If this were a location that they routinely visited, then it would be cleared of overgrowth, show signs of recent habitation. That it remains undisturbed and unkempt could very well indicate that it is indeed a place that they currently shun."

"This here cave," Jarrod continued. "It reeks of power—cantcha feel it? We'd be a damn sight safer taking our chances with them savages outside than we'd be stayin' in here for even another second longer."

Ofelia snorted in disgust, her silhouette barely visible in the dimness. "If I had not talked you into hiding here, we'd both be dead right now," she pointed out.

Stepping between them, I raised a hand, attempting to ward off any potential arguments. "It no longer matters why we entered," I said. "Now that we're trapped, we need to find out how far back this place extends, look for another exit."

Xavier searched through his pockets and then came up with the flashlight he'd used earlier. Scanning the interior, he revealed the nearby web-festooned walls and ceiling as we all blinked against the sudden illumination.

"Aren't you concerned that they'll see the light?" I asked.

"Yes, but they already know we are in here," he retorted. "And they seem to have no desire to follow. I think it is safe enough. For now. As your friend has so eloquently pointed out, they are afraid of whatever is in here with us. So let us just go and take a look at what is lurking back there in the shadows, shall we?"

His levity was as forced as his fleeting smile, a thin veneer covering his mounting anxiety. Yet there was nothing to be done but push forward. In my mind, if there was any way that we could get out of this mess, I was going to find it. Retrieving my cell phone from the waterproof pouch at my belt, I joined its light to Xavier's and began looking around.

The cave had once been entirely natural, but generations of artisans had carved and enlarged it. They had also covered most of the walls with elaborate Peruvian motifs. Stylistically, they were crude, but the detail and amount of work put into them was astounding. The looping, rounded figures of animals and people were joined by an interwoven pattern of greater complexity. And incorporated throughout the entire design were the symbols familiar to me from the Mi-Go map tile fragment I still carried.

Knowing these carvings dated back thousands of years did nothing to alleviate my growing puzzlement. Instead, it only strengthened my suspicions that the Mi-Go had somehow influenced these people in a multitude of mysterious ways. As we moved deeper into the darkness, I once again marveled over the thought that an alien race could have had contact with an indigenous tribe here without it ever being noted before.

What intergalactic secrets had been revealed to the ancient inhabitants, what exobiological wonders had they been a party to those many long years ago? Thoughts swirled through my mind, speculations and ideas with very little factual information backing them up. Shaking my head, I decided that our current dilemma was more important than trying to figure it all out. So, using my cellphone to light the way, I moved farther into the darkened gloom before us.

After a short distance, the floor became tiered on three sides, creating four levels leading down to a central area. As I descended into the middle of the main chamber, I directed my light toward the far end, discovering a platform heaped with an overabundance of priceless offerings. An idol sat at the center of this pile of riches, and to either side were placed large, rounded bundles of intricately woven textiles. The craftsmanship of the ancient Peruvians was legendary, and their weaving of complexly patterned cloth was beyond compare. Yet just what were these strangely wrapped artifacts laid out next to the central figure? I had nary a clue as I stood studying them in the light of our various devices.

"Mummies," Xavier supplied, shining his flashlight upon the mounds of exquisite fabric. "My ancestors would prepare their dead for the afterlife, decking them out in valuables before arranging them into sitting positions and then wrapping them in many layers of fine cloth. During certain events, they would be unwound and their honored relatives brought forth to join in on the festivities. Just who these particular people were, I do not know. But judging by the level of workmanship involved in this tomb's creation, and by the valuable offerings stacked around them, I would have to say that they were probably all once highly respected individuals."

This information caught me off guard. Up until now, the only mummies I was familiar with were of the Egyptian variety. Yet here was an example of that ancient embalming technique that I had not previously been aware of, and it was one that I immediately found immeasurably fascinating. But I could not let myself be distracted by these moldering antiquities while such a foreboding idol sat tall and menacing at the far end of the room. It was truly an astounding piece of work and so intimidating to look upon that it captured all of my unwilling attention.

Fashioned in the semblance of an ancient Incan warrior, it wore an elaborate fan-shaped headdress and featured deep-seated emeralds for eyes. But its stern visage and lavish accouterments were not what drew my unwavering regard. For coiled completely around this imposing figure was a huge serpent, its body carved to perfection, with a lumpish head overlooking the idol's right shoulder. It was this blunt-snouted horror that mesmerized me, its hideous countenance facing outward to seemingly stare at us as we approached.

As I stopped a few feet away to study the elongated skull, beady eyes, and the squarish gash representing its mouth, my companions gathered around the pile of tributary items below it. And while Xavier and Ofelia knelt to further investigate the offerings, Tunuhun maneuvered his way behind the effigy, seemingly more interested in what lay beyond than in the trinkets heaped at its base.

"Imaitchuq—sumiitpa aasi?" he said, glancing back at me.

Coming closer, I gazed at what was resting on a raised platform just behind the idol. There, littering the floor, was a collection of vibrant fabrics and other wrappings, obviously the tattered remnants of funerary cloth, lying in a heap along with a scattering of other personal effects that might have once been held securely within.

"Shouldn't there be a mummified body inside this?" I asked Xavier. "It looks like someone ripped this one open to get at the valuables. Could grave robbers have been in here at some point, do you think?"

Xavier came to take a closer look, followed by a noticeably perturbed Jarrod, whose eyes continuously scanned the chamber with ill-concealed fear. Joining his light to my own, Xavier peered down at the shredded cloth, his features overshadowed with confusion. "This has not been ripped into," he said, running the light all across the fragments. "It looks to have been torn open from the inside out."

"Dios mio!" Ofelia breathed, her eyes wide as she joined us. "How can that be?"

Tunuhun reached out to run his fingertips along the edges of the pile, then held them up. They glistened wetly in the flashlight's beam with a slime that wasn't immediately identifiable. Using hand signals, I indicated that he should scout around and then turned to scan my cell phone's light more thoroughly throughout the rest of the room's interior. As the artificial illumination penetrated all the darkened corners, Tunuhun stepped over the pile of treasure, his hand straying to the pistol holstered at his belt.

"If this one exploded from the inside out," I said to Xavier, "wouldn't there be bone fragments and pieces of desiccated flesh? What would cause one to blow apart like this? Trapped gases?"

"I do not know," he replied thoughtfully, still studying the remnants of cloth and other debris. "Generally, the bodies would have been carefully prepared with all of their organs being removed. There would not have been anything left which could have caused any sort of buildup of gases. So an explosion seems unlikely. And yet, as you have just noted, where then is the mummy? There are no signs of the body that once inhabited these wrappings, no remains that would indicate there was anything ever resting within to begin with."

Tunuhun was just making ready to move beyond our immediate circle of light when there came a series of metallic chimes echoing out across the stillness. Something had fallen near my foot, striking the stony floor and then bouncing away. Aiming my light at the dusty ground, I was able to track the motion of the small object as it rolled to a stop.

It was an elaborate earring, glistening with a wetness which caused the gold and silver to shine even more brightly in the cell phone's radiant beam.

Kneeling in the dirt next to me, Xavier nervously glanced around, clearly perturbed by this unexpected event. Ofelia stood with a hand on his shoulder while

Jarrod flattened himself against the back wall. Tunuhun simply slid into a defensive crouch, his muscles tensed and ready. Then, as one, we lifted our various devices to shine their light upon the ceiling above.

In the shadows spread across the cavern's roof was a mass of something heaving as it slowly undulated. It appeared to have many limbs, like a prehistoric sea anemone intermixed with the body of a gigantic centipede. And as we stared up at this eldritch horror in stunned disbelief, the torso of a mummified tribal chieftain uncurled from a niche in the ceiling, opening its dead-white eyes to peer down upon us. Then, stretching wide its blackened maw, it uttered a raspy hiss that was more insectile in nature than any sound a normal man could ever make.

With a startled cry of abject terror, Jarrod crammed himself into a crevice in the rear wall, and we all quickly followed suit, sliding and scraping ourselves raw as we shimmied sideways into the slender opening. It was a tight fit, and soon none of us could even move another inch. I was the last one in, and I pivoted my head around sharply, aiming my light back out into the room we'd just vacated.

"Jarrod!" I wheezed out, my chest compressed by the rocky walls. "Can you go any deeper?"

"No," came the shrill response. "I'm stuck! There ain't no way outta here—it's justa dead end, a fissure in the wall with no other exit!"

As this information sank in, the creature before me slithered down off the ceiling, dropping in loosely segmented coils festooned with tentacles and other chitinous appendages. This multi-limbed abomination then reared up in front of the crack, the torso of the mummified Peruvian serving as the thorax of its hellish centipedal body. And as its cold, dead eyes glared at me, it hissed again, an alien sound that set the hairs on the back of my neck to standing on end. With a sinking feeling in the pit of my stomach, I also noted that just beyond it, to either side of the burial chamber, the rest of the round bundles of textile cloth had begun rocking back and forth. While we were trapped, compressed between the rocky walls of this forgotten tomb, they had begun sprouting legs and wavering tendrils as the horrors within sought to emerge from their ancient funerary incubators.

8

The walls on either side were gouging into my flesh, crushing me between thousands of pounds of earth and rock, and the compression was so great that it left me struggling for air. With our cell phone lights now awkwardly positioned, the indirect illumination showed me only indistinct glimpses of the terror pursuing us. But that was enough to provoke a sickening sense of dread, which spread quickly throughout my entire being. As the malevolent creature scuttled forward, I could see that the layers of its rubbery flesh were oozing a repellent mucus, its mummified head and thorax heaving with these glistening secretions as it drew nearer. And in the shadows beyond this hideous monstrosity, the other textile-wrapped bundles were now bursting apart, loathsome, insectile legs thrusting through the ancient cloth as the desiccated corpses within mysteriously transformed. Being closest to the outer edges of the fissure, I could not escape as the nearest one thrust its arms into the crack, gripping the jagged stone on either side with razor-sharp claws. Then, drooling a thick, repulsive slime, it leaned forward until the horrific, shriveled features of its desiccated face were mere inches from my own. What little breath I had left caught in my throat as I was momentarily paralyzed by its looming proximity.

The torso of this amalgamation of insect and man was a withered husk now made animate by some unknown force. Yet I could see fluids rapidly coursing through the spidery network of its prominently exposed veins. As these rigid, blackened tubules bulged outward from the contours of its wizened flesh, they were pumping it full of renewed vigor. Its eyes, dark as a moonless night, stared into my very soul as its lower jaw cracked open, widening far beyond the strictures of any living mortal man. Shockingly, this gaping gullet was filled with small, pointed teeth, layered like those of a prehistoric shark. And as its rotted tongue lashed out, I was sprayed with globs of its viscous, reeking saliva.

Gagging, I fumbled for my sidearm, benumbed fingers grasping blindly as my trembling hand scraped painfully along the walls of the fissure in a fruitless, scrabbling search. But as I groped frantically after the weapon, the thing's slavering lips retracted even further, exposing more of its serrated denticles in a series of uneven, circular rows. Then, with piercing, bone-jarring shrieks, it began snapping savagely at my face. By sheer luck alone, the brutal attack was hindered by the close-set walls, its morbidly distended jaws flaring far too wide to fit within such a narrowly confined space.

Rearing back on the coils of its centipede-like lower trunk, it hissed in frustration, a sound not unlike a fat dollop of lard hitting the bottom of a heated iron skillet. Then, thrusting more of its spindly, insectile arms into the crevice, it heaved at the outer edges, attempting to widen the gap by sheer brute force alone. The lashing tentacles sprouting from its back shot forward as it struggled, wriggling wetly across my trembling limbs as they sought to find purchase enough to pull me from my place of refuge. Deprived of oxygen, unable to retreat or even reach my sidearm, my life suddenly flashed before my very eyes. In a fit of delirious terror, I jerked helplessly back and forth, trying desperately to escape from the thing's relentless persecution.

The walls themselves were shaking violently, a testament to its supernatural strength, and a flood of dislocated earth suddenly poured down from above, filling in the crack as it buried us alive. Ofelia screamed over Jarrod's harsh sobbing, a heart-wrenching combination, while Xavier cursed loudly in Spanish. Tunuhun was babbling in Inuit, but I could not hear the words clearly, could not fully grasp the significance of what he was saying. My attention was solely focused on the scene now playing out before my unwilling eyes. Within the burial chamber, the newly emerged entities were scuttling around chaotically while my antagonist's tentacles had somehow managed to wrap themselves around my quivering limbs. But then, with a sound like a mine shaft collapsing, the walls abruptly drew apart, giving way to the unnatural power of the creature's unwavering efforts. And as more rocks and dirt rained down, I felt the floor beneath me disintegrate, sending us all sliding backward into an unknown abyss. The grasping tentacles were torn from their tenuous hold on me as my own body weight carried me away into the void.

For a few moments, we were entirely airborne, plummeting through open space as the chamber above us swiftly receded. Then we landed hard, rolling pell-mell down an embankment until we slid to a stop in a pile of shale, dirt, and battered bodies. Around us, the earth was still quaking, and in the wavering light of our cell phones, I saw that rubble continued to spill from the ever-widening crack as the thing redoubled its maddened efforts. Flinching away from this horrifying sight, I tried to redirect my cell phone's sporadic illumination even as those behind me cursed my clumsy fumbling. Yet I had to know, had a sudden, irrepressible urge to perceive the immediacy of our approaching demise. For I knew then that if even one of the repellent beings followed, we'd be torn apart and consumed by these mummified warriors so recently reborn as demonic centipedal life.

As the fall of debris tapered off, my redirected light revealed the worst of my fears. The fiendish entities were now scuttling through the widened gap en masse, covering all sides of the newly formed opening in a writhing glut of squirming, nausea-inducing motion. We were surely done for, but my mind rebelled against our impending doom, leaving me struggling frantically against the detritus still covering my lower extremities.

Then Xavier was there behind me, thrusting his arm out over my right shoulder. In his fist, he clutched a handgun, and he repeatedly fired this weapon, not at the advancing horde but at the shuddering ceiling instead. With a thunderous eruption, the entire burial chamber collapsed, crushing the foul creatures beneath tons of crumbling rock. And as a landslide of rubble crashed down to bury us even further, we scrambled to drag ourselves free from the cascading debris.

Managing to regain our footing, we staggered drunkenly away, putting some distance between ourselves and the accumulated wreckage. The hillside we were trapped beneath then quivered with a series of aftershocks, rumbling violently before falling eerily silent. Panting in unresolved terror, we stood staring blankly at each other in the feeble light of our battered devices, finding ourselves now lost within these unknown Stygian depths.

After a moment, Xavier began checking Ofelia over for wounds while Tunuhun dusted off his clothing, shrugging to loosen his massive shoulders. Jarrod simply collapsed to the ground in a disconsolate heap, sniffling back tears. But aside from some minor bumps and bruises, we appeared to have come through the unsettling event relatively unscathed. It was a miracle we hadn't been killed. Or worse. And yet, we were now stuck here without supplies or any real knowledge of our present location. In an attempt to gain a better understanding of our whereabouts, I rotated my light around in a wide arc, illuminating everything within our immediate vicinity.

The large, natural cavern was perhaps a hundred feet across, although it was hard to calculate its full extent as I could not completely see the outer sides. Water was dripping somewhere nearby, a familiar sound that was strangely comforting. And massive stalactites hung down from the roof to join with protruding stalagmites, forming a maze of mineral-streaked pillars. My comrades were shaken, but they had already regained enough of their composure to realize the gravity of our situation.

"What were them things?" Jarrod asked in a quavering voice. "I ain't never seen nothin' like that afore."

"I do not know," Xavier replied, his arm clasped protectively around Ofelia's shoulders. "But I think that whoever made them will soon be hunting us. We should find a way out of here before they send more."

Shaking off her brother's comforting touch, Ofelia glared at me, a flash of anger creasing her dirt-streaked features. "I do not know what the hell is going on here," she spat, "but Xavier is right; we need to get the fuck out of this hole and then make our way back to the boats. There is nothing worth dying for in these godforsaken lands. We should leave the indigenous people to their secrets and then never return! It was a mistake to even come here at all!"

She had a point, but the trauma of our near-death experience was clearly impacting her mental stability. "They'll have found the boats by now," I advised softly, seeking to ease her growing hysteria. "We should try to make our way to the spot indicated on the Mi-Go's three-dimensional map instead. Their technology is very advanced, and we might find something there that we can use to fight our way back past that tribe."

"You and that stupid map!" she exploded, stepping forward to jab her rigid forefinger into the middle of my chest. "This is all *your* fault! The only reason we are even in this mess is because of you and that accursed chunk of rock. And what is your answer to all of our problems? Kill more of my people! What kind of a monster are you? You come here, desecrate our lands, and then decide to wipe out anyone who stands in your way. You're no better than the Spaniards! You people take and take and take, always grinding away at our national pride and independence. Well, here is something that you can chew on, *cabron*—I am done listening to you and all of your metaphysical bullshit! I don't care who your uncle was or what he did for us; from here on out, my brother and I will lead this expedition. And I say we head for the river. We need to get out of here before any more of those things show up. Can't you see that they are somehow a part of the local ecosystem, perhaps even the ancestral guardians of this place? We need to leave now and never look back!"

Xavier gently pulled her around to face him. *"Querida hermana,"* he said tenderly. "Calm yourself. We need to stay together, now more than ever. If we try and go back to the river, we will be captured and most likely killed. Besides, we still have to work our way free of this cave before we can do anything else. And in order to do that, we need to stick together."

"So you are taking his side over mine now?" she exclaimed, shoving him away with madness in her eyes. *"Que!? quieres que sigamos siguiendo a este idiota?* He is not one of us, does not even know the ways of our culture. Without our help, he will not even make it back to Iquitos! We should be in charge, you and I, together. We have the skills needed to navigate the surrounding jungles safely; these others—they are all just dead weight! I cannot believe that you are choosing these gringos over your own flesh and blood!"

"No one is taking sides," he reasoned. "It is just common sense to do what he wants for now. We may know how to survive in these jungles, but as you say, these people are helpless. Would you truly leave them all here to die? Once we find the Mi-Go hive, then we will have a secure base to start from, a place from which to navigate our way back to safety. That tribe was afraid to come near the burial chamber, and that means those reanimated hybrids were not controlled by them, not placed there by our ancestors. Whoever set those guardians is our enemy, and they are the ones who have defiled our lands. They might even be minions of this Nathrotep, the same being who is controlling the minds of our government. You want to see them punished for their crimes, right? Well, if we head toward the river now, we not only doom ourselves to failure, but we will also never discover who is behind the desecration of that tomb. We cannot let them get away with whatever it is they are doing here in our country. Can you not see that?"

"All I can see right now is my own brother betraying me!" she cried tearfully, sobbing in frustration.

Enfolding her in his arms, Xavier stared at me over her bowed head as she wept disconsolately against his chest. His eyes spoke volumes, yet I did not fully comprehend why he was backing me up, nor what he hoped to gain by doing so. But I was not one to look a gift horse in the mouth, so I nodded in acceptance of his support, then saw him dip his chin a fraction in response. The only thing I was really certain of right now was that he was entirely correct—we needed to stay together if any of us were going to get through this alive.

Glancing at Tunuhun, I saw that he was simply awaiting my orders. Steadfast as always, my trusted friend believed I would make the right decision for us all. But in the shadows cast by the wan light of our cell phones, I could tell that holding back the spirit of Ezra was taking its toll. His face was beaded with sweat, his eyes sunken from resisting the undead warlock's ongoing attempts at possession. Yet there was nothing we could do about that right now, and I needed his expertise to navigate our way clear of this mess. So, with a hand signal, I let him know he should start scouting around. Nodding almost imperceptibly in acknowledgment, he knelt, studying the ground. It struck me then that we would soon run out of power; cell phones were notorious for having a short battery life, especially while using the flashlight app. We had to find a way out quickly or risk being trapped here in total darkness forever. It was not a comforting thought.

Considering our surroundings, Tunuhun stood and then reached into his pocket to pull out a butane lighter. Having no idea what he was about to do with it, I patiently waited, watching as he ignited it before holding it up above his head. In the open air, the flame flickered, wavering from side to side, then bent backward slightly. Satisfied with the results, Tunuhun extinguished the flame, then moved off in the opposite direction, following the breeze he had just discovered. Where there was wind, there had to be an opening somewhere it was coming in through. Admiring his ingenuity, I motioned for the others to proceed and then knelt down next to Jarrod.

"How are you holding up?" I asked.

His features were pale, jowls quivering with barely suppressed fear, yet he tried to put a bold face on it. "I been better," he said. Then, as he accepted a helping hand from me, we stood together, staring at each other in the dim light. "I don't trust none of them others," he suddenly whispered. "There's somethin' fishy goin' on. Mark my words!" Shaking loose dirt from his clothes, he then turned to follow the rest of our companions as they walked away into the surrounding gloom.

We traveled for what seemed like an eternity, always following the slender hint of a breeze, which soon became a stronger waft of air, then a humid draft filled with the fragrant scents of jungle vegetation. The path we followed wove in and out of interconnected chambers, steadily sloping downward, and in several places, we were forced to descend sections of porous rock or crawl through tunnels barely large enough to fit through. But as our cell phones began to fail, we finally came upon an area where moss was growing along the floor and the thunderous sounds of a waterfall could be heard through the thick walls surrounding us.

Following the sound, we eventually glimpsed a faint natural light coming in through a distant opening. With a way out seemingly close at hand, we made for this glimmer of freedom with an enthusiasm that briefly overcame our almost total exhaustion. Climbing over boulders slick with beaded moisture, we worked our way forward until we came to a ledge situated next to a raging waterfall overlooking a vast jungle canopy. It appeared as though we'd made it through the tunnels alive, yet where in the hell were we? As rays of golden sunshine slanted down through the overhanging foliage, I gazed upward, trying to determine our exact whereabouts.

From what I could tell, we were at the bottom of an immense crater or crevice running along the floor of the Amazon jungle, a place sunken so deep between overgrown cliffs that it must have gone entirely unnoticed by the scientific community. There had certainly been no indication of it on Huxtable's maps, and he definitely would have mentioned it had it been a known feature of the surrounding geography. I guessed that it had to be closer to midday by now for light to have even penetrated this deeply. As the mighty waterfall crashed down and rainbow-hued mist swirled around us, we stood staring out in wonder over the hidden world that we'd inadvertently discovered.

The view was spectacular. Yet we were now standing at the lip of a precipice, shivering with exhaustion and bereft of supplies or even a means to call for help. Ofelia and Xavier knelt at the edge of the falls, cupping their hands under the cascading water to get a much-needed drink. But Jarrod simply sank wearily to the ground, mopping sweat from his balding head as Tunuhun observed the fog-shrouded landscape below us. Searching the towering walls above, I saw that there would be no escaping in that direction. We did not possess a rope or any other means to ascend safely, and tackling such a sheer slope without them in our weakened state was out of the question.

Directing my attention back to the rocky slopes, I sought a way down into the forest, a path to possible safety from the elements. We needed to find food and shelter soon, then we could perhaps plan our next moves. As I stood surveying the cliff face, the radiational fog hugging the vegetation beneath us parted under the warmth of the sun's glowing rays. And as its ever-expanding light traveled slowly across the treetops, it exposed a faint glimmer of reflected radiance in the far distance. Narrowing my eyes, I peered in wonder at the magnificent sight now revealed in all its unexpected glory. It was a city of some kind, its buildings and temples shimmering with glints of gold in the afternoon sunlight. Like the famed ruins of Machu Picchu, this walled and intricately laid out series of structures was built in the style of the ancient Inca. Yet its buildings were all in perfect repair, with a series of cultivated terraces carved into the hillside around it for farming and agriculture. It was a miracle beyond anything I'd ever hoped to find here.

It then occurred to me that whoever lived there would not be overly welcoming to strangers appearing unannounced. A thriving community secluded in the depths of the Peruvian jungle was likely to want nothing to do with the outside world, least of all me and my band of weary travelers. But without any better options presenting themselves, this city of the lost was now our only hope for total salvation.

9

After careful consideration, we made our way down the slick-sided slope, scrambling precariously over boulders covered with glistening moss saturated by the waterfall's misty spray. I was surprised to find that the jungle's curved elevation rose up to merge with the lower part of the cliffside, thus providing us a shorter route through the canopy below. Proceeding into the verge of the forest, we stuck close to the churning river at the base of the waterfall, making our way toward the settlement we'd seen from above. And within a few moments, we came upon a small clearing nestled beside a back eddy pool swirling endlessly at the water's edge.

The scientific community would have been overjoyed to find this hidden ecosystem as it was populated with specimens I'd never beheld elsewhere. In the first few minutes alone, I had already spotted several butterflies and monkeys that were completely unfamiliar. But I couldn't let myself be distracted by such wondrous biodiversity. We were in a tough situation, and I needed to focus all my attention on our immediate survival.

"Our first priority should be to find food," I said as we paused to rest. "We don't know what kind of reception we'll receive at this mysterious city, and the natives here could prove to be hostile."

Ofelia's mouth twisted into a sneer of contempt. "That just shows how ignorant you are. My people are a peaceful race, at one with the world around them. For all we know, whoever lives in that city will welcome us with open arms. Why do you automatically think that they will harm us?"

"Ever since setting foot in these jungles, we've been attacked at every opportunity. So, in this case, I would prefer to err on the side of caution."

"That is a very narrow-minded way of viewing things," she countered. "Both of those previous tribes were obviously manipulated by outside forces and then forced to act in self-defense. I firmly believe that if we approach this new community in a peaceful manner, then we will be treated differently."

"You're not being very realistic," I groused, irritated by her futile bickering. "Look, all I'm saying is that based on what little information we have, caution would be the better choice. We don't know how these people are going to react to our sudden appearance, so we should try and observe them from a safe distance before revealing ourselves."

"My brother and I have far more experience in these matters, and yet we've spent this entire trip listening to you. And just look where that has gotten us! You really have no idea what you're doing here at all, do you? In fact, without us, you'd already be dead!"

"Um, guys?" Xavier broke in.

"What?" we both shouted, rounding on him.

"I do not think you need argue any further as it seems that we have already attracted their attention . . ."

Glancing at the surrounding jungle, my eyes grew wide in shock. For from within the depths of the forest, figures had begun to reveal themselves, slipping quietly through the foliage from every direction. They were short and wiry, painted in orange and gray pigments, with bright spots of coloration daubed in circles upon their foreheads and cheeks. Even though armed with spears and bows, they appeared more curious than hostile, gazing at us with unfeigned wonder. But then a hooded figure stepped out from the trees at the opposite end of the clearing. Barking an order in what I presumed to be the tribe's own dialect, his commanding tone had an immediate effect. With visible hesitation, the spears and arrows were raised and then reluctantly pointed in our direction.

The man giving the orders was definitely not a native. Dressed in elaborate vermilion vestments, he looked like a blood-drenched bishop, his garments standing out in stark contrast against the lush backdrop of surrounding greenery. As he moved toward us, his body swayed in a curiously languid motion, and when he finally stopped to lower his cowl, his strikingly blue eyes gazed at us from out of a gaunt and irregular skull. I shot Tunuhun a sharp glance of reproach for not warning us, but he merely shrugged, indicating that he hadn't been aware of their approach. Putting his failure down to not being overly familiar with our new surroundings, I returned my attention to the stranger, who was now studying us with a look of shrewd calculation.

The temperatures, even this far down in the depths of the crevasse, were excessive. And although it was somewhat cooler next to the river, all of us were sweating profusely, our clothes drenched with perspiration. But the heat and humidity seemed not to affect this bewildering individual. Instead, he appeared impervious, the skin of his shaven head not even beaded with a single drop of moisture. It was uncanny. And as he saw me staring, his lips, a thin, cruel gash dividing the lower half of his face, twisted into a sour smile. "So, you are Gillam," he murmured. "And this must be your associate, Tunuhun." His narrowed beady gaze swept across us, eyeing my companions from top to bottom. Then, with an unimpressed grunt, he motioned to his entourage. "Bring them," he commanded.

After confiscating our weapons, the natives herded us into the jungle, thus beginning an arduous march down overgrown pathways. I tried questioning our captor once and received the butt end of a spear jabbed into my ribs for the audacity. There was no doubt in my mind that we were being led to the structures glimpsed from above, but for what purpose I could scarcely fathom. The only certainty was the fact that we were once again being held against our will, and it rankled me to no end. I was growing very weary of being treated as a pawn by those who thought themselves more powerful than I and longed for the day when we could strike back. Yet that day was not today, and there was no sense in getting ourselves killed before we could even determine who our newest adversaries were.

The sun continued its lateral movement across the sky as we walked along, dipping beyond the upper edges of this immense rupture in the jungle's floor and casting everything into a preternatural twilight. It struck me that this must be an everyday occurrence as the sun's radiance could only penetrate these depths during certain times of the day. Even so, the plant and animal life here flourished in these unique surroundings, as they were perfectly suited to this primordial environment.

I had read about a similar location being discovered once before, and the scientists who had stumbled across that particular sinkhole had uncovered a plethora of new species which existed nowhere else in the entire world. It was places like these that often encouraged divergent evolutionary paths, and it made me wish that I had more time to study this peculiar habitat. But we were prodded along at a ground-eating pace until we finally reached the city at the end of the sunken valley.

Even though my knowledge of the Incas was spotty at best, I could tell that the structures here were built in the style of that once-mighty civilization. The dwellings were all crafted from huge blocks of stone, precisely fitted together and then decorated with animal motifs done in bold bas-relief. They were primarily single-story structures, with the exception of a grand step-sided pyramid looming at the very center. And there were many additional signs of prosperity on display here as well: gold plating and scintillating gems encrusting the walls and adorning many of the carven figures dotting the numerous plazas we crossed.

I realized then that this mythical place must have resided here untouched by outside influences for perhaps millennia. Untouched except by those who ruled here now, these red-robed figures who were clearly in charge yet obviously not native to these lands. Just who were these intruders, and what were they doing governing a tribe that had existed unmolested for untold eons? The conundrum continued to vex me as I openly studied the inhabitants filling the streets around us.

For the most part, they appeared healthy and fit, wearing finely woven textiles and embellishing themselves with other precious accouterments emphasizing their wealth and status. Yet there was a dourness hanging about them, a thinly veiled resentment reflected in their flat expressions as they surreptitiously watched us pass. I could sense a growing animosity festering here, an unvoiced hatred of these foreign overlords, accompanied by a deep, carefully concealed fear.

Seeing them at close range, I was struck by a sudden epiphany. Judging from their body paint and style of dress, this was the same tribe who'd attacked us on the river two nights ago. What had they been trying to accomplish when they'd swarmed our boat, and why? And what of the strange powers they'd been wielding? Apparently the influence of the red-robed overseers went beyond mere subjugation. There was much going on here to puzzle over, yet no obvious answers as we were herded along. Upon reaching the terraced fields on the opposite side of the city, we were taken to an area where a multitude of bamboo stockades had been erected.

They were built like the pens made to hold dangerous beasts but contained familiar-looking captives instead. Members of the other tribe from last night were locked away here, yet I had no idea why. If these two tribes were indeed working together, then why had these warriors been detained? Perhaps Ofelia had been correct in assuming that they'd only been protecting their territory, but that seemed too convenient an explanation. They had savagely attacked a group of heavily armed men with little or no regard for their own personal safety. Protecting your territory was one thing, but such an act of unbridled violence was suicidal. So what then had driven this particular tribe into such a frenzy of bloodthirsty destruction? The more I thought about it, the more confused I became. As my frustrations grew, we were led to the largest stockade at the end of the row and then forced to wait while the robed leader unchained the gate.

After the elaborate padlock and chain had been removed, we were prodded into the grubby pen, the man's beady eyes gleaming as a brittle smile played across his thin-lipped mouth. Without another word, he then resecured the entrance before turning away. "Wait!" I shouted. "Why are you holding us prisoner? We are not your enemies!"

Pivoting to glance back over his shoulder, he studied me with pursed lips, his gaze roving over us as if we were some sort of prized livestock. "That remains to be seen," he stated cryptically, then glided away between the rows of stone buildings, moving off toward the temple. Shaking my head in consternation, I turned to take stock of our situation.

In the perpetual twilight of these hidden lands, I hadn't at first noticed the other occupants of the cage trapped here with us. Surprisingly, it turned out to be the remnants of Jon's mercenary band slumped in various positions of dejected defeat. Seeing them made me wonder why they'd been captured at all instead of simply killed. As for myself and Tunuhun, I knew that we were most likely wanted for questioning. We were obviously known to our hosts, and they were perhaps even familiar with our true mission. That led me to consider the ramifications of this foreknowledge. If they knew about our quest to find the Mi-Go hive, then what else might they be aware of? And more importantly, just what did this information mean to them? Were they also looking for the technology that the Mi-Go base was sure to conceal? I had no idea who these robed figures were, but it was almost certain that they did not wish to use the ancient artifacts for altruistic purposes. Their true intentions remained clouded in secrecy, at least for now.

Turning from my silent musings, I bent my thoughts back to the problem at hand. We were all suffering from a lack of sleep and sporting a myriad of cuts and bruises. And our weapons, including the ancient book Jarrod had kept in a waterproof satchel, had been confiscated when we were taken prisoner. The cage itself was unbreakable, the lock devilishly complex. Besides that, there was really nowhere we could escape to, even if we had the means. This deeply sunken rift in the jungle's floor was surrounded on all sides by steep, unscalable cliffs.

Yet the other prisoners, both tribesmen and wounded mercenaries alike, had been brought here sometime before our own arrival. So there had to be another route down through the bluffs, one that would take us back to the surface more expeditiously. We merely had to determine where this secret pathway was hidden and then make use of it without getting caught. It was a tall order, and one fraught with such peril that it would take all of our not inconsiderable talents in order to achieve it. But as I stood staring at my bedraggled companions, my hopes dwindled away into nothingness. In our current condition, we wouldn't be going anywhere, and that was a fact that I could not simply ignore.

Jarrod, his face streaming with perspiration, suddenly leaned back against the bamboo bars, sliding to the ground in total exhaustion. Just to his left, Xavier stood quietly conversing with Ofelia while Tunuhun simply regarded me with unperturbed interest, awaiting my orders without visible concern. His undiminished trust in me suddenly lent me strength. If he had no doubts about our chances, then why should I? Straightening my spine, I took in a deep breath and then began assessing our options more optimistically.

That we hadn't been killed outright spoke volumes. Whoever our captors were, they wanted us alive, at least for now. And that led me to consider why. The man who'd detained us had known our names, or at least the names of myself and Tunuhun, so it must have something to do with our mission. But who else besides the five of us knew what we were really after? Dr. Huxtable was one, and perhaps some of his staff back at their main camp, but that was about it.

Jon and his team knew very little; they had come with us out of revenge, not to find the Mi-Go hive itself. Other than that, there was my aunt up in Alaska and the government black-ops team that was hellbent on tracking us down. The people ruling here were definitely not American agents. There had to be some other explanation. The archaeological staff had left with the other boat while Jon and his soldiers had been with us the entire time. So just where had our captors gotten their information? Turning to Xavier, I cleared my throat, intruding upon his private conversation with Ofelia.

"Who else knew about our venture back in Lima?" I asked. "Besides you two, who else could have learned about what we were trying to do here, what we are seeking to find?"

He considered a moment, eyes shadowed with unease as he stood deep in thought. "I told no one else," he finally stated. "I have no idea how these strangers could have found . . ."

"It was that stupid little cunt!"

The spite-filled interruption echoed ominously from the back of the cell, immediately drawing our attention to the collection of wounded men stationed there. Shoving his way roughly through this group of dispirited individuals, Jon limped over to where we stood, his battered features a livid mask of pure, unadulterated rage. "I saw her leaving the camp last night right before the attack. She's the one who told these savages where to find us. She brought this down upon us all! We should kill the backstabbing bitch right where she stands. Kill her and leave her here to rot with the rest!"

I gazed at him in shocked disbelief, studying his maddened expression in the unnatural twilight. Clotted blood covered his face while his outfit was torn in several places from the intensity of battle. In addition, I noted that his right arm was bound in a makeshift sling while a puncture wound on his left shoulder continually oozed blood through a filthy scrap of bandage. Yet it was his eyes that drew my unwavering regard as they were red-rimmed and filled with such feverish intensity that it went far beyond mere justifiable rage. Here was a man delirious with unbridled anger, someone who'd clearly been pushed well beyond the boundaries of rational thought.

And what's more, he was probably right.

My gaze slid away from him to settle upon Ofelia where she stood within the protective circle of Xavier's arms. She really was the only one who'd left the camp last night, the only person who'd had the opportunity, and the motive, to turn us in to the indigenous population. And as she saw this realization dawn upon me, she shivered in reaction, shrinking deeper into the confines of her brother's sheltering embrace.

10

"You're going to want to rephrase that, *pendejo*," Xavier murmured, moving to stand protectively in front of Ofelia. "That's my sister you are talking about. And if anyone is to blame, then it should be me; I was the one who scouted the area and failed to identify the danger. Ofelia had nothing at all to do with the ambush."

"Then maybe we should just kill the both of you!" Jon snarled, his bloodshot eyes filled with madness. "If it wasn't for your incompetence, my men would still be alive and our mission a success! I knew we shouldn't have trusted a couple of ignorant savages to scout the way forward. You fucked us real good, you stupid son of a bitch!"

It was ironic that the mission he spoke of was one in which we'd planned on destroying the very same indigenous tribe who'd assaulted us. Yet this did not seem an opportune moment to point that out. Some of the other mercenaries had started to cluster together in a sullen mob. Bruised and battered, these soldiers had little left to them now except for misguided revenge. And this was made abundantly clear by their resentful muttering, a low, feral sound which filled the air with the promise of impending violence.

"I would like to see you try, you *pinche psicopata*," Xavier spat. "It looks like you already got your ass kicked pretty hard last night; in your condition, I could probably knock you out without even trying."

Eyes widened with indignity, Jon let out a strangled cry, his one good fist raised to strike. But Tunuhun lunged forward, catching the man's wrist in an unbreakable grip. For a few seconds, Jon strained against the hold, but Tunuhun just stared him down. And then, as suddenly as he'd lashed out, Jon deflated, shoulders slumping in defeat. Seeing this, Tunuhun loosened his grip, and the man yanked his arm away. But his followers were further incited by this mistreatment, their simmering rage boiling over as they prepared to overwhelm us.

"Everyone, just hold on a second!" I shouted. "In case you haven't noticed, we're all trapped here together, held captive by a common enemy. The worst thing we can do right now is fight amongst ourselves. We need to conserve energy for an escape attempt."

Jon's lucidity slowly returned, his eyes taking on a calculative squint. He was a pragmatic man, a survivor of many confrontations on various battlefields. And he was no fool. "He's right," he shouted, turning to face his comrades. "It doesn't matter whose fault it is right now; the only thing that really counts is making it out of here alive. After that . . . well, I make no promises as to what will happen once we're free." His gaze swiveled back to focus on Xavier. "You and I are not through here," he said with a scowl. "We'll settle this at another time."

"I look forward to it," Xavier responded, his expression grim.

As the men sized each other up like two huskies squabbling over a scrap of salmon, a loud snore erupted from inside the cage. Already spun up from the near confrontation, we all jumped at the sound, eyes drawn toward the source. Jarrod, clearly exhausted from the previous night's ordeals, lay curled up on the ground, head pillowed on his meaty forearms. Having slept through the entire encounter, his snores were now deep rumbles of blissful ignorance. With this interruption, the tension in the cage evaporated, everyone growing envious of his peaceful slumber.

"We need to gather what's left of our strength," Jon finally stated, studying Jarrod with a self-deprecating grin. Turning, he called out to his men. "Alright, everyone! Let's settle down for a little siesta, shall we? We'll want to be well-rested when those red-cloaked bastards come calling. I'm so goddamn tired right now I can't even think straight. Randle! You have the first watch. Wake us in an hour or so, and then you can sleep while the rest of us figure out what to do." Turning back to me, he raised an eyebrow. "That sound alright with you?"

This did not seem like an ideal place for a nap. But gazing at Jarrod slumbering on obliviously, I decided that it made little difference in the long run. The men in charge of this Incan city would come for us either way, and there was really nothing more to be done about it right now. So, nodding in agreement, I turned to my own companions.

"He's right," I said. "There's no telling what's in store for us, and we need to be ready for anything." None of the others looked happy about it, but it made sense to rest while we still could. Scanning our surroundings one last time before bedding down, my attention was inadvertently drawn to the adjacent stockade.

The captives there were a rag-tag bunch, just as injured and desolate as we were. Huddled together, they stared back at me with expressions of hatred and condemnation. Just who were these aboriginal people? And why had they attacked our camp when their true enemies were obviously the foreigners controlling this city? The answers eluded me. Shaking my head in frustration, I sat with my back against the bamboo bars, telling myself I would only doze off for a few minutes.

With a start, I regained consciousness, feeling a nudge at my hip from someone's boot. For a moment, I was unsure of where I was, the images of a strange dream still permeating the reality of the waking world. There was something there in the depths of my slumbering mind, a visitation of sorts. A powerful woman, a group of astral crusaders, something about a rift in time and space. But then it was gone, tattering away like mist before the rising sun. Rubbing my eyes to clear them of sleep, I glanced up to see Tunuhun standing over me. Catching my attention, he made the hand signal for danger, then pointed across the compound to a group of cowled men who were now steadily approaching.

Darkness had fallen, but it was being kept at bay by torches carried by the cultists in the formation. They marched together in lockstep, their robes fluttering as they moved in unison, voices raised in a sonorous cadence that was punctuated by the jangling of shaken bells. Incense braziers were swaying to and fro, held by men at the front and back of the entourage, the pitted metallic censers ancient and well used. Through a whirling miasma of acrid smoke they came, the chanting droning on in a continuous litany with a guttural response at the end of each stanza. It was in no language I'd ever heard but reminded me faintly of Latin.

The leader of the procession was tall and menacing, the shadows of his cowl completely obscuring his features. Moving into position in front of the cages, they split apart, forming two equal units. Within the stockade beside ours, I could see the tribesmen shrinking away from these hooded figures, apparently well aware of what was coming next. Seeing their reaction sent fresh chills racing down my spine. Clambering to my feet, I stared at the head cultist, who was now standing silently between the two groups.

His robes were the same coloration as the man who'd captured us earlier, yet gilded and embroidered with complex patterns along the hem and sleeves. The stitchery gave me pause, teasing my eyes with its glowing serpentine configuration. But then, his deep, resonant voice called out the final stanza of the chanted verse, his followers giving their one-word response in a hollow, echoing shout. With the censers still billowing and the torches lighting the darkness with a flickering radiance, the men took on a much more sinister aspect. Swallowing heavily, I approached the bars of the cage in fearful anticipation.

The moment stretched on, the silence deepening, and we all seemed to hold our collective breaths. Then, with a slow, almost glacial movement, the leader reached up to draw back his cowl, revealing gaunt features in the surrounding torchlight.

His bone structure was wide and flat, the flesh stretched as if the skin didn't fit well over the underlying skull. I wondered if the condition was something that came from privation, perhaps some type of ailment developed from the rigors of an austere life. Whatever the cause, his visage was downright unsettling. Studying the man further, I decided he was much older than our original captor, perhaps even older than Jarrod. But his eyes, the same intense blue coloration, were filled with a similar amount of bored indifference.

Raising both arms, he motioned with his hands, a distinct directive to his gathered brethren. Splitting off from each group, two of the younger acolytes came forward to unlock the chained doors, gesturing for the occupants within to exit. With a slow caution that illustrated our cumulative fear, we all shuffled hesitantly out into the courtyard, huddling together within the circle of light. One of Jon's men in particular was having a hard time of it.

Wide-eyed and favoring his injuries, the soldier swiveled his head about like a terrified rabbit, peering into the darkness on all sides as he trembled uncontrollably. Then, without warning, he bolted, fleeing toward a nearby alleyway. But before he'd even made it more than a dozen steps, a long tendril of rubbery flesh whipped around him, jerking him high into the air. With a shrill scream, he disappeared from sight, and then a series of blood-curdling cries immediately followed. The despairing reverberations of his torturous wailing were soon cut short as the echoes of crunching bones and torn flesh reached us from out of the shadows.

As we listened to him being devoured, any further notions of escape were swept aside by the sobering thought of ravenous beasts patrolling the streets. If I had wondered about the lack of guards before now, then surely here was my answer. These men did not require any human counterparts to keep us in line; the monsters pacing the byways around us were all the deterrent needed.

Glancing over at Jon, I half expected him to go berserk, to demand an accounting for his lost man. But his eyes were filled with terror just like the rest of us, his belligerence stifled by the overwhelming threat of danger. Meanwhile, the tribesmen being rounded up from the adjacent cage were strangely silent, their faces exhibiting the dead-eyed stares of people who'd already been condemned to death. It was an unsettling observation which did nothing to quench my own rising dread. It seemed that there was little any of us could do now to evade whatever fate awaited.

We were quickly formed up into two lines, each surrounded by a half dozen cowled figures with every other cultist holding a burning brand. Once so arranged, the procession started off through the warren of avenues, the torchlight barely holding back the all-encroaching darkness as the robed figures once more took up their chanted refrain.

It was strange to be marching through this ancient Incan city in the dead of night. The carvings and gold-plated statues soon took on a more sinister aspect, the wavering flames of our escorts' torches revealing mere hints of the culture that dwelled here. Yet as I shivered in reaction to the unsettling situation, I found little room left for idle speculation. Fear ruled us now, and it was a feeling shared by all as we were herded along amidst the hellish chanting and the incessant jangle of primordial bells.

Eventually, we came upon a plaza situated before the centralized temple itself. This towering structure was clearly visible because of huge, well-lit braziers set up around its perimeter and also placed upon each of the wide steps leading upward. Thus illuminated, the pyramid was truly an awe-inspiring sight, its outer appearance strongly resembling fortifications built by the ancient Incas when they were still at their full height of power. Yet even though it had many of the same features as a conventional pyramid, the temple was still vastly different from the one we'd seen inside Nathrotep's pocket dimension. While it was obviously constructed out of stone cut from the surrounding cliffs, it also included tall archways with wide trapezoidal doors made from unfamiliar materials. It was quite impressive, even though the destination itself left much to be desired. I did not know what we were in for once we entered this foreign mausoleum, but whatever was in store, it could not possibly be to our benefit. With these morbid thoughts still swirling through my mind, we were ordered to a halt just outside the main entrance.

The leader, his severe features distorted in the surrounding firelight, stopped his recitation of the Gregorian-style chant, then issued a series of directions to his disciples. Following these orders, his sycophants separated out some of the captives, creating a third group at the base of the steps. It was then that Jon roused himself enough to finally protest.

"Now wait just a goddamn minute!" he exploded. "Where in the hell do you think you're taking my men?" Behind him, there was a sudden rumble of agitation as the other mercenaries began pushing back against our oppressors.

In response to his outburst, a loud hiss echoed through the air, accompanied by movement from the shadows around us. Within seconds, two hideous creatures materialized, scuttling forward to flank the head priest on either side. His expression of disapproval was a daunting scowl that would have stopped lesser men dead in their tracks.

In the brazier's blazing radiance, these unholy guardians were now fully revealed. Here were the same type of creatures we'd seen in the tomb last night, yet subtly different in many ways. The desiccation of mummified remains was gone, replaced by strapping torsos of living men combined with the unusually large centipedal bodies. From the backs of these foul beasts sprouted a myriad of appendages similar to the lappets of a jellyfish, and these loathsome tentacles lashed through in air, their slender lengths dripping with noisome fluids. Additionally, the segmented lengths of their lower extremities were capped off by vicious-looking pincers, while each multitudinous leg sported claws the size of a harpoon's spearhead.

But the most frightening aspect of the abominable amalgamations were the men who'd been melded into these grotesque morbidities. Their bare chests glistened with a sheen of repellent slime while the immaculate paint once gracing their savage features was now congealed like the drippings of a melted candle. A new swath of pigment had been applied across their foreheads, a muddy gray streak which caused their jet-black eyes to stand out in vivid contrast. Added to this was a series of fresh yellow spots trailing down their necks like the markings on a poisonous tree frog. I knew not what they were, but my body responded by quaking in uncontrollable fear, my legs wobbling as I struggled to remain upright in the face of such damnable horror.

The people clustered behind me were faring no better. I could hear their low moans of abject terror, smell the fresh stench of urine as a few even lost bodily control. Here were nightmarish conglomerations they'd never before seen, as it was only my companions and I who'd witnessed similar monstrosities the night before. Yet even though that experience had not steeled my nerves against their frightful appearance, I couldn't help but wonder about their origins. They must have come from somewhere, and I was betting that they'd been created by whatever mysterious cult now controlled this city.

A bark of incongruous laughter broke through my racing thoughts, causing me to seek out the source of this unexpected joviality. Jon stood highlighted in the fluctuating flames, his mirth a sure sign of his ever-slipping sanity. Taking a step forward, he shook his fist at the cultist leader, his eyes bright with fevered intensity. "Your pets don't scare me," he brazenly announced. "If you were going to kill us, then you would have already done it by now. So tell me where you're taking my men, or by god, I will beat your face in with my bare hands!"

There were sharply drawn breaths and gasps of astonishment all around at this brash statement. Even Tunuhun's normally placid features shifted into a look of calculated surprise as he considered the possible outcome of Jon's ultimatum. But the man in charge was undaunted, his icy expression not even wavering. Into the ensuing silence, there came the distant dissonance of shaken bells, punctuated by more insidious chanting from unfamiliar voices. Our attention was immediately drawn to the upper heights of the great pyramid itself. And from the top of that astounding monument there then came a procession of intricately decorated tribesmen marching down in synchronized order.

These individuals were adorned like the ones who'd attacked the boat two nights ago, clearly residents of this hidden jungle community. Gray paint was smeared across their foreheads, with yellow spots of pigment trailing down their necks. In addition, bangles of bronze, silver, and gold decorated their arms along with a myriad of colorful feathers. Upon reaching the courtyard, they proceeded to form a rough circle around us, dancing about in wild abandon. Their chieftain appeared last, holding a slotted, long-handled board covered in small bronze bells. When he shook this device, the others cried out in guttural response. And once they had us completely surrounded, the leader stepped over to Jon, glaring up at him with a look of fierce displeasure.

Jon sneered at the smaller man, opening his mouth to utter something sure to be laced with poisonous contempt. But he was cut off as the chieftain shouted out a single, power-filled phrase:

"Karta-shokka-ka!"

Instantly, Jon went rigid, his body trapped within an atmospheric conjuration closely resembling a globe of ball lightning. Hair standing on end, he spasmed fitfully, bright arcs of electricity sizzling across his flesh. The chieftain then shook the bells once more, calling out to his men, and they took up the haunting refrain. Etheric energy pulsed outward from them, enveloping us all in a web of sorcerous power that stunned with the intensity of its vibrant assault.

It was a sensation not unlike being trapped between two Tesla coils, the electrical current running over and through each one of us as we stood immobilized within its electrostatic grip. Just when I felt that my frazzled nervous system could take no more, my insides cooking under the onslaught, the cultist leader raised his hand. Seeing this, the chieftain shouted a command, and as quickly as it had begun, the traumatic event ended.

While everyone was still partially paralyzed, the tribesmen gathered together the other indigenous captives, along with most of Jon's remaining soldiers. This new group was then herded up the temple steps toward its apex, an area now wreathed in a shimmering violet light. With an almost casual gesture from the cultist leader, his acolytes took control of those that remained, leading us through the trapezoidal entrance and then down into the bowels of the temple itself.

Those left from the original group included myself and my companions, along with Jon and several of his mercenaries. It was with this reduced party we were escorted deeper into the depths of this imposing edifice, past rooms filled with unsettling sculptures and along corridors decorated with intricately carved Incan motifs. After several minutes of walking, we were eventually ushered into a rectangular chamber at the very heart of the fanciful structure.

The room itself was sparsely decorated, featuring two large, rectangular pools of water running the length of a central walkway leading toward the back of the room. Light was provided by roaring braziers gracing the corners, along with torches set at intervals across the room. The exquisite bas-relief chiseled along the upper portion of the walls was amazingly detailed, showing scenes of Incan people sacrificing men and women to an ancient serpent god. Yet all of my attention was immediately focused upon the man seated behind a grandiose desk, a piece of furniture clearly out of place amongst the rest of the minimalistic Incan decor.

He was well aged, perhaps in his late sixties or early seventies, but that did not detract from his radiant vigor nor the composed elegance of his brooding personal magnetism. He was currently entering notations into a large, leather-bound book, his concentration wholly absorbed by this small menial task. As he worked, the light of the braziers gilded his short, silvery hair with highlights of amber and gold, spilling across the embroidery of his elaborate crimson vestments in glistening waves. After a few moments, he closed the book with a snap and then glanced up, his bland expression unreadable upon crisply shaven features.

"So," he said at last into a silence broken only by the crackle of brazier flames, "you are Gillam from the Last Frontier, then? I must say that while your notoriety does precede you, I am distinctly unimpressed by your physical presence here within my domain."

11

The man stared at me, his face set into almost imperceptible lines of strained tolerance, and I could not help but wonder who this stately, well-spoken gentleman was. And what exactly was he doing here in an Incan city lost within the depths of the Peruvian jungle? He was obviously the cult's leader, but his red-robed minions were entirely unknown to me. And as he studied us with his piercing, unblinking gaze, I racked my brain to come up with something to say that would not immediately result in all of our deaths.

"I am indeed Gillam," I began cautiously. "But how did you come to know me by name?"

His expression never faltered, yet there was a slight crinkling of flesh around his eyes that bespoke of perhaps an infinitesimal emotional reaction. Folding his hands together, he leaned back in the chair, still looking at me as if I were a bit of offal to be scraped from the bottom of his shoe. "How could I possibly not know?" he stated. "You and your companions have been traveling around for the past week causing staggering amounts of chaos. You don't even have the faintest idea of how you're really going to deal with the various forces that you've unleashed, do you?"

My mind was awhirl with thoughts and emotions. How did he know of our misadventures? The things we'd done, places we'd discovered, the creatures we'd inadvertently awoken? Here was someone who evidently had knowledge beyond my current understanding of our situation. If I played my cards right, could I not perhaps gain some advantage by drawing this information out of him? With no better options presenting themselves, it was certainly well worth a try.

"We do have something of a plan," I hedged. "It's one of the reasons we're here now. We are seeking a specific location hidden within these jungles, a place that predates any of the civilizations that have sprung up in this area over the last several thousand years."

"Ah, yes," he sighed. "The Mi-Go hive. I know all about it, and I'm also intimately familiar with the book your porcine friend there was tasked with protecting, a tome of ancient spells and rituals that Nyarlathotep is now so very eager to obtain. Not to mention the map tile fragment you so audaciously pilfered from that primordial base in the Brooks Range." Waving a languid hand, he indicated the items, which now lay on the corner of his desk, taken from us when we'd been captured.

"But I am curious," he continued. "What exactly did you intend to do once you'd uncovered this newfound installation? How did you hope to breach its defenses, to enter its hallowed halls which have been sealed for perhaps hundreds of thousands of years? Surely you weren't hoping that Nyarlathotep would somehow magically appear and deign to help you? That madman couldn't even help himself, let alone assist you malcontents in your ill-advised plot to stop the Mi-Go invasion. Just what did you think you were going to achieve here? Honestly, your strategies are so transparently nonexistent that it boggles the mind. You don't really have any plan of action at all, do you? You're just randomly wandering from one place to the next, causing immeasurable damage wherever you go. Frankly, I'm surprised that you haven't gotten yourselves killed during any of the encounters you've initiated thus far."

As his words sank in, I felt my heart grow heavy. He was right. We really had no plan beyond the desire to stop what we had already set in motion. There was no grand scheme, no concrete, finely detailed agenda to get us out of the messes we'd made. We were just stumbling from place to place, making things worse the further along we got. A cloud of self-doubt settled around me like a funerary shroud, casting all my high hopes and aspirations into the dust.

"We didn't ask for this," I said defensively. "We were forced into it. What would you have me do? Stand idly by while our world is overrun? At least we're trying to fix our mistakes. Once we gain entry into that nearby Mi-Go base, we hope to find technology we can use against the forces being sent from their home planet, perhaps even thwart Nathrotep's mad ambitions. Beyond that, it's hard to say. Instead of criticizing our ineptitude, why don't you offer to assist with our efforts? You seem to know a great deal about what's going on; why not use that knowledge to help us prevent a war that will surely destroy the entire planet?"

"Yet you did have a choice, though, didn't you?" he accused. "You *volunteered* to investigate that Alaskan hive, you and your friends, practically forced your village elders into allowing you to go. And for what? To prove that you know what's best for your entire community? To show them there are better ways of doing things outside of the ancient traditions followed by your own people? Your arrogance is astounding. Did you actually think that you're smarter than the oldest members of your tribe? Simply because you went off to attend college and came back filled with a sense of intellectual superiority? I can tell you right now that your elders were right; you should have waited, should have held out until that team of black-ops agents took command of the situation. Now you have those very same agents chasing you around, cleaning up after you, when you should have let them deal with it all in the first place. They could have stopped the Mi-Go from ever leaving this planet. In fact, if you hadn't interfered with the newly awoken nestlings, forcing them to contact their leaders across the depths of time and space, then there wouldn't even be a pending invasion to contend with.

"And what of your inexplicable decision to go to that unnamed town," he continued relentlessly, "seeking out a person whom you'd never even met, a madman by all accounts, whose dabbling in the arcane arts has left him bereft of all reason? What did you hope to gain by that? An ally? Perhaps someone knowledgeable enough to translate this trivial map tile fragment that you've somehow placed all of your hopes upon? The idea is preposterous. Just look at what that foolhardy decision has resulted in. Now Nyarlathotep, or 'Nathrotep' as he's chosen to call himself this time around, has gone to ground, hiding himself away in an unassailable dimension that not even my Brotherhood can infiltrate. Your meddlesome interference has destroyed years of hard work by my order in pinpointing our adversary's movements, delaying all our carefully orchestrated actions against him. What did you hope to achieve by provoking the mad god like that? Did you think it would go differently? Did you even consider the consequences? Somehow, I think not."

Leaning forward, his intense, unblinking gaze bore into me. "But all is not lost," he offered persuasively. "I have indeed decided to help you, to relieve you of your burden. All you need do is to tell me how you were planning on opening the nearby Mi-Go hive once you'd found it. Then my Brotherhood and I will take the necessary steps to prevent all the catastrophes you have thus far unleashed. You and your friends can board the next flight home, forget about what you have seen, and live out the rest of your mundane lives in relative tranquility. What do you say? Are you prepared to let me assume the responsibility?"

His observations and accusations cut me to the core. Yet deep in my heart, I knew he was right. Everything we'd been through was my fault. If I hadn't felt so sure of myself, hadn't talked the elders into letting us go to that mysterious new pinnacle that had thrust itself up out of the permafrost within the Brooks Range, then none of this would have happened. Those agents would have gotten to the hive in a timely manner and prevented the Mi-Go from ever leaving the planet.

And going to the unnamed town had also been a huge mistake. We had achieved nothing tangible, and the end result was my best friend being possessed by the spirit of an undead warlock. Not to mention the chaos we'd caused by interfering with Nathrotep's agenda. How could I have ever believed we'd be able to nullify the combined threat of an alien invasion and the desires of a deranged demigod commanding an army of hybrid ghouls?

As I dwelled upon all the misguided decisions I'd made leading up to this point, I became increasingly morose. This entire trip was a fool's errand. Now that the stakes were so very high, maybe I should just give this man what he wanted and leave the rescuing of our world to people who were better suited for it.

But before I could offer up a reply, Jon shook free from his partial paralysis and stumbled forward. Bracing himself on the edge of the desk, he glared down at the cult leader, his face twisted in rage. "Just who the hell do you people think you are?" he ranted, his muscles still quivering from the electrified spell. "You can't hold us here. By detaining us, you're only setting yourselves up for a world of hurt. The rest of my men in Iquitos will track us down and then descend on this place like a swarm of heavily armed locusts. They should be here any time now. But if you play fair with us, tell us what we need to know, and then let us all go free, I'll consider calling off their attack. What do you say, old man? Do we have a deal?"

"Pitchuġ iiyautaitchut," Tunuhun murmured in my ear while the two men stared each other down.

His whispered comment about a missing key made little sense at first, but then, it suddenly dawned on me.

What was the one thing this priest desired, the only reason that we were even still alive in the first place? He wanted access to the Mi-Go hive and thought we had the means to unlock it. His whole persistent cajolery, his strained tolerance of our very presence here, was based solely upon the belief that we could breach that portal. His Brotherhood wanted nothing more than to enter the ancient base themselves. And he cared not one whit whether we lived or died once they obtained this information. His offer to take responsibility and send us all home was a sham, a thinly veiled lie to induce us into giving up secrets that I did not even have. We still had an edge here, if only I could find some way to exploit it.

While I stood pondering this new train of thought, he raised one hand, indicating to his waiting followers that he would handle the situation personally. Then, still locking eyes with Jon, he rose from his seat, gathering up the book and tablet fragment from the corner of the desk. "You dare to dictate terms to me? We are the Brotherhood of Asklepios, an ancient order of scholars and physicians! Our primary task is to collect and catalog all the lost knowledge of the world while building a better understanding of the healing and metaphysical arts. Do not deign to challenge me, boy, for you are woefully ill-prepared to deal with what you might unleash."

Jon smirked, regaining some of his hubris as he shoved away from the desk, standing tall and menacing in the flickering light of the burning braziers. "Now you're just trying to scare me off," he insisted. "I've seen your layout, witnessed your so-called 'Brotherhood'; there's not a trained fighter here among them. And your overall defenses are pathetically nonexistent. Once the rest of my crew gets here with the heavy artillery, your followers won't stand a chance. So you better come clean and make a deal before I lose my patience."

I found Jon's arrogance rather impressive, yet knew his boasts were just a ploy. There was no way his soldiers would ever find us in this uncharted rift cleft into the jungle's floor. It would take them far too long to even locate this hidden valley, let alone pinpoint our exact position once they did so. No, we were on our own here, and his bravado, while it did have a delaying effect, would get us nowhere. I opened my mouth to intercede but was cut off as the high priest responded.

"I understand your willingness to try and browbeat me into submission," he said. "But you are forgetting one thing: the Baratusi. They are the direct descendants of the once mighty Incas, and this is their land, their city that you are currently standing in. Did you never wonder if the other members from your excavation site ever made it back to Iquitos? The Brotherhood and I have a mutually beneficial arrangement with this indigenous tribe, you see. The god they worship is very similar to our own, and we have built up a lasting partnership with them over the years. So consider this: If that other boat of yours were to somehow become lost with all hands, then who would be left to tell the rest of your soldiers where to look? The only people who truly knew your original destination are standing right here in this very room. So, before you try strong-arming me, you best consider the position you are in here. There is no one coming, no well-armed squad of would-be rescuers descending upon this settlement to free you. All your puffed-up chest beating is nothing more than a paltry front, a toothless, weak-minded bluff intended to manipulate me into capitulating."

"If that's true," Jon replied bluntly, "then why are you keeping us alive? The way I see it, you would have already killed us by now if you didn't need me to negotiate with the rest of my team."

At this statement, a small, brittle smile briefly cracked the cult leader's stoic expression, making him seem even more predatory in the flickering firelight. "And there you are wrong again," he said. "We have need of healthy specimens such as yourself for reasons that are better left unmentioned. Besides, we've already negotiated a preliminary deal with one of your associates, and we are holding to the terms of that arrangement. If nothing else, our word is our bond, and we stand by it."

Jon's eyes flickered to where Ofelia stood with Xavier's arm protectively encircling her shoulders. Glaring daggers at them, he suddenly swelled up with impotent rage.

"I knew it!" he finally exploded. "That little bitch sold us out!"

Just then, a scream from above us split the air, trailing down through the stone walls behind the desk, ending with a huge splash like the sound of a whale breaching. We all froze, glancing at one another in shocked surprise.

"You *really* want to know why we need you alive?" the man asked, his eyes shining in the light from the roaring braziers. "Follow me, and I shall enlighten you."

Motioning for the acolytes to bring us along, he turned from his desk and pushed on a decorative stone carving. With a pivoting motion, a section of the wall swiveled open to allow access into the room beyond it. And as we were ushered into this new area, we were greeted by the sight of one of Jon's men flopping helplessly about in a gigantic circular reservoir set at the center of the chamber.

The body of water was immense, its boundaries defined by a low stone wall surrounded by elaborate statues placed at equal distance from one another. All the statues depicted serpents entwining columns of fluted diorite, their finely sculpted heads overlapping the top and positioned to face the central pool. In the middle of the ceiling directly above was an opening slightly smaller than the cistern below it. From our vantage point, we could see an altar emitting a blazing violet light and the be-feathered tribesmen gathered around it, along with the rest of the remaining captives.

Lit only by the eldritch illumination seeping down from above, the hidden area was wreathed in shadows. But as we watched, a beam of pale moonlight broke through the clouds in the sky to slide across the pond, gradually bathing it in a shimmering glow. As the moon's brilliant image graced that immense reservoir with its glorious visage, something stirred beneath the surface, causing ripples to distort the luminous reflection. The man treading water cried out, desperately trying to swim to the edge. But he was suddenly pulled under, a smooth coil of that submerged leviathan briefly breaking the surface before sinking back into its blackened depths.

"The god of the Baratusi lives within this sacred cenote," the high priest said. "It has dwelled here for generations, refreshed by the waters of the Amazon, which are connected to this temple through a series of underground conduits. The Baratusi honor their god by offering it living sacrifices on a regular basis. Many such subjects are required in order to keep it satiated, and they continually raid the nearby villages to take what is needed. In exchange, they believe that these sacrifices grant them good harvests, strong children, and healthy livestock, among other less tangible things. So you see, we do need you for something other than a bargaining chip for negotiations. Your men provide us with fodder for their jungle deity, and at no cost to us. For that is also a part of our deal; we provide fresh captives from outside sources to help them sustain their god's hearty appetite."

Struggling to keep his composure, Jon swallowed heavily, his gaze now locked upon the rippling surface of the water-filled cenote. "Why do you need the rest of us down here then?" he asked. "Why aren't we . . . why aren't all of us up there right now?"

"Because that is the other side of the bargain," the man said smoothly. "My Brotherhood also requires strong, able-bodied men such as yourself for our own purposes. The jungle tribes in these parts provide us with a population to draw from that will never be investigated. And in return, we choose subjects to feed to the Baratusi god from miles around, ensuring that this resource is not depleted before it can repopulate. The Baratusi don't mind the condition of the extra sacrifices we bring them: homeless inebriates, beggars, lost children—all go to feed their ravenous god's appetites. In this way, we can supply them indefinitely while they provide a base for our own operations. It is a mutually beneficial arrangement that we find to be most satisfactory."

"That still doesn't explain what you need us for," I broke in. "Why are we here, besides providing you with the correct way to open a Mi-Go vault?"

"Because you have done what no other person in the history of our Brotherhood has ever accomplished—you have infiltrated a Mi-Go base and lived to tell the tale. We not only need your expertise in opening the one we have here but also your thoughts and observations on what interacting with them and their technology was like. We've dealt with those of their contemporary brethren here on Earth many times over but always as adversaries and never within a hive the size and configuration of the one you found. We hope that the sealed base here will be of similar technological magnificence, perhaps providing us access to scientific wonders that these space-faring creatures possessed thousands of years ago. Your willingness to give us this information will not go unrewarded, while we also intend to honor the agreement our agents in Lima made with a certain member of your entourage. As for the rest of you, such as your robust security chief here, they will go on to be used for . . . other purposes."

Thinking it through, I doubted that Tunuhun or Jarrod could have had the time to make any side deals while in Lima. And I also trusted them implicitly. However, one of the two siblings who'd joined us upon our arrival may have had the opportunity. But what sort of deal had been made? And what would become of us once the leader of this Brotherhood of Asklepios discovered that I had no idea how to unlock the hive they were so determined to enter? The outcome was painful to consider, and my mind shied away from it.

Hoping for an epiphany, I let my eyes wander the room, and much to my surprise, I saw a small, feline face staring out at me from behind one of the statues on the far side. Focusing my full attention upon it, I was only able to catch a fleeting glimpse of a fluffy tail as it scampered off into the shadows. It made me briefly wonder what a domestic cat could be doing here in this ancient Incan temple.

A chanted shout of Baratusi language accompanied by incessantly shaken bells interrupted my thoughts, and then, another man was cast down through the hole in the roof, his scream echoing around us as he fell. From out of the depths of the pool, a massive ophidian creature rose up, its jaws opening wide and snatching the man from midair before plunging back into the pond, causing waves to slosh over the raised edges. This god of theirs was very real, a gigantic serpent of some kind by the looks of it. And as its grayish-brown coils disappeared beneath the waves, I had to restrain myself from falling to my knees in debilitating terror.

The high priest grinned slightly, seeing my discomfort, then motioned to his men, indicating they should bring us along as he headed for an archway on the far side of the room. Wherever it was he was taking us now, I knew in my heart that there would be no escape and no plausible way we could strike a deal which could possibly set us all free.

12

"W-wait . . . wait just a minute, here . . ." Jon stammered while we were being ushered along. "If you can just stop feeding people to that . . . that thing, then maybe we can strike a deal. You said you needed men. Well, I have a whole squad, and they're heavily armed. If they're not already on the way here, then I can arrange for them to come to us. It's obvious you need people around you who know how to fight. And for the right price, I can offer my team's services. All you have to do is stop killing us long enough to discuss the details!"

He was grasping at straws, and even I could hear the desperation in his voice, feel the fear rolling off him in waves. But I knew that there was no way this austere leader of the Brotherhood of Asklepios was going to make a deal with him. And this was made abundantly clear as the priest simply ignored his pleas, leading us across the room without further comment.

Passing through the darkened arch on the opposite side of the sacrificial chamber, I felt my body tingle and go numb for an instant, as if being exposed to subzero temperatures. Then we were through and standing in a new area that was set up like some type of elaborate laboratory. It was massive in size, far larger than could have fit within the confines of this underground temple complex. Glancing back through the archway behind us, I sought to confirm that we were even still in the Baratusi structure at all. But the entranceway was now covered by a shimmering vortex, much like the one Nathrotep had used to seal his ghoul city, Gul'Nictolanthropep, off from the real world. I could only surmise that we had once more been transported into another pocket dimension. Refocusing my fractured attention, I studied our new surroundings with stunned disbelief.

This immense, rounded enclosure with its surrounding colonnades and domed roof reminded me strongly of a Greek tholos. And as light blazed in from above us, I saw that the dome itself was a fanciful work of stained-glass art, featuring intertwining serpents cavorting across its many brightly colored panes. Yet the main floor below it was jam-packed with tables covered in scientific equipment while complex machinery I did not recognize ran from floor to ceiling along the rounded walls. Hanging from support beams above it all were also a series of fluorescent lights spaced throughout the room, further illuminating the tables beneath. To our right, part of the floor was taken up by archaic bookshelves crammed with tomes of all shapes and sizes while on the left, there were a multitude of tube-shaped tanks laid out in crowded rows. With a bad feeling growing in the pit of my stomach, I saw that half these containers were already filled with tribesmen and mummies, seemingly held in some sort of chemical suspension.

Yet the most terrifying thing about the room, the sight that set my teeth on edge and had me quivering with barely suppressed revulsion, was the other denizens inhabiting that vast chamber. Here, there existed examples of the Brotherhood's most spine-chilling servitors, a veritable cavalcade of human-insect hybrids that scuttled about while unmodified acolytes worked the tables. As I attempted to bestill my racing pulse, I noted that they were predominantly the centipedes with human torsos we'd witnessed earlier. And many of them were simply clinging to the walls above the machinery in a living carpet of grotesque, segmented bodies and multiple chitinous limbs. The high priest caught me staring and favored me with a small grin.

"We are primarily an academic Brotherhood," he stated proudly, "but we have also reestablished many lost metaphysical procedures over the years, combining them with modern-day scientific advancements. Here we have found that the fusion of the *scolopendra gigantea* with a human upper torso makes for a more mobile and tactically offensive organism, even while using the mummified remains of the dead. We have perfected this technique with the resources we have at hand and established many other production facilities around the globe as we prepare for our own god's imminent rise. Unlike the Mi-Go, or that maddened fool Nyarlathotep, we seek to cohabitate with the rest of humanity after subduing them. We will make this a world where all will see that our god is the only logical choice for everlasting worship and veneration."

Walking around one of the nearby tables, he smoothed his hand along its cold, sterile surface, his face taking on a musing, almost bliss-filled appearance as he envisioned his cult's plans for the future. "Over time, the Baratusi have assisted us greatly in this. As we have indeed given them much knowledge in return, as well as helping them to subjugate all of the other undiscovered tribes currently living in the Amazon. With these undocumented resources at our beck and call here in the Americas, along with our legions of centaurpedes, we will soon establish a new utopia, one that will extol the virtues of our deity alone."

"Just who is this god that you speak of?" I asked, dreading the answer.

"Why, Yig, of course," came the surprised response. "I thought that much would be obvious by now, seeing as how we are so closely aligned with the cryptid the Baratusi currently worship. You see, our god is a benevolent one, the father of snakes and all other serpents, and also fiercely protective of his children. So, the mighty river deity of this hidden Peruvian tribe is under his direct protection and guidance. In fact, we have come to take on many of the same characteristics as their serpentine godling. Its powers are compatible and much favored amongst my kind now, especially here, in the jungle."

His explanation was mostly lost on me, although I did not allow my confusion to show by any outward sign. Just who was this 'Yig,' and why did these people worship him? I had no easy answers. All I knew was that we had once more stumbled across yet another plot to conquer the Earth. Were we doomed to uncover every foul sect on the planet while searching for a means to stop the evil we'd already unleashed? My spirits, severely dampened from the priest's earlier observations of my ineptitude, sank to an even lower degree. What the hell was I supposed to do now? I knew nothing about this Yig and only slightly more about the other two factions aligned against us. How in the hell were we going to stop the Mi-Go from invading, defeat Nathrotep with his army of ghoul hybrids, and now somehow prevent this serpent worshiping cult from taking over the world?

"What does that have to do with any of us?" I asked, curiosity overcoming my rampant fear. "If you are currently unbeatable with your armies of modified beasts and subservient tribesmen, then why would you even need the secrets hidden in an ancient Mi-Go stronghold?"

"Finally, I am rewarded with a glimmer of intelligence!" he exclaimed, although his facial features barely registered the enthusiasm. "Allow me to elucidate further. The fact of the matter is, now that you've stirred the other players into a frenzy by your ceaseless meddling, we need an edge, an advantage over our adversaries in order to ensure our success. I cannot have the Mi-Go invasion force, or the chaos inspired by Nyarlathotep's machinations, endangering our plans. Since you have so prematurely awoken them to action, we must now work harder to combat their influence, build upon our own strengths, and recruit others who will do our bidding out in the real world. And that being said, I am reminded that I have a promise to fulfill."

Fondling the ancient book and map tile fragment he still carried, his gaze swept over us with an expression of haughty benevolence. "One of your party members has helped us immensely by bringing your arrival to our attention, allowing us to orchestrate your every move, while also leading you unerringly to us. I must admit that it was a little touch and go there when our plan to finally capture you was thwarted by your escape into the tunnels below the tomb we'd prepared. But things worked out in the end. So now, we offer this individual the rewards they requested as payment for their invaluable assistance. This exceedingly rare book, *Charmides Treatise on Mystical Maleficence,* and the map tile fragment as a gesture of our continued goodwill. We will honor the bargain our agents struck back in Lima, and more. Here—take these as a token of our appreciation. But if you would be so kind, we will still require a copy of its contents for our own edification . . ."

He held out the items, and all eyes were drawn toward the person they were being offered to. Standing in the protective circle of her brother's arms, Ofelia's eyes widened as she grasped the full import of the high priest's words. Swallowing heavily, she shrugged away from Xavier, taking a tentative step forward. But then she rounded on her brother.

"*Mi hermano,*" she cried. "How could you!"

A wave of emotions crossed Xavier's features, alternating from surprise to confusion and then to an anguish so deeply felt that tears sprang to his eyes. He gazed at his sister imploringly, his lips trembling and brows furrowed, and the love he felt for her was a palpable thing. But then, he mastered himself, shaking free of the devastating inner turmoil, before resolutely crossing to where the priest was standing. Accepting the book and map tile fragment, he gazed down at his prize, caressing the worn leather of the book's cover. Then, straightening his shoulders, he faced his sister with an air of grim resolve.

"I did this for you . . . for us!" he rationalized. "With the power and knowledge contained in this book, we can do more to help our own people than anyone else in the history of our entire country. Just think of it—if our ancestors had held the power hidden within these pages, then the conquistadors would never have subjugated them, would not have been able to brutalize, rape, and pillage throughout our lands. With the Brotherhood on our side, and aided by the forces they control, we can end the persecution of our fellow Peruvians, break the hold that Nathrotep has on our elected officials. We can finally take back what is ours and put competent people in place to control and moderate our own government. It is what you have always wanted, what we have always dreamed of. There was no other choice; I had to make this arrangement . . . for the both of us."

"There is *always* another choice!" Ofelia cried. "This is not what I wanted—this is . . . barbaric! The Brotherhood's entire plan is insane, and these dark arts are forbidden. We were to find other ways of stopping the mad god from controlling our leaders, not this! Your betrayal and your willingness to use that horrid book are unforgivable!"

"This family squabble is very touching," Jon cut in sardonically, "but what about my men?" Turning back to the priest, he waved his undamaged arm toward the archway behind us. "You are wasting a valuable resource by feeding us to that thing out there. These fucking monsters you're creating, they're impressive, I'll give you that. But they can't think like a real soldier, can't know the strategies of war like I do. With my team at your disposal, you'd have a military-trained strike force backing you up, not just these brainless zombie drones."

Sweat dampened his brow, and he had a wild look in his eyes. Behind him, his men were abjectly terrified but remained silent. All of them were out of their depth in this situation and looking to their leader to save them. But the priest was unimpressed by Jon's wheedling, his features as stoic as ever in the well-lit room.

"You make an excellent point," the older man observed, his robes rustling as he moved to stand just in front of the tall security chief. "And that is why I have chosen you and these few others—your knowledge will enhance the capabilities of our constructs immeasurably."

Waving his acolytes forward, he motioned for them to take charge of Jon and the rest of his soldiers. There was a brief struggle, but the high priest put an end to it with a short but powerful incantation. At this arcane utterance, a field of electricity embraced the combatants, causing them to freeze up. With Jon and his men stunned into compliance, they were then led over and placed into separate tanks. Once this was accomplished, the robed minions returned to surround our reduced party once more. And with an air of superiority, their leader then moved to a control panel situated at a centralized work station.

"Now you will serve us as our god intended," he intoned, manipulating the controls.

There was a whine of energy, and then the canisters filled with a greenish liquid, clouding up the glass and obscuring the occupants within. A series of lights at the tops of each container blinked down from red to yellow, and there was a groaning sound accompanied by a whoosh of air escaping as steam billowed out from the base of each tank. When the mist evaporated, the tubes contained creatures made from combining the upper torso of each man with the lower segments of a gigantic centipede. Doors opened to allow these newly made servitors to scuttle out and join others like them that were already swarming across the upper walls beneath the stained-glass dome.

"How did you . . . how could you possibly make these things?" I sputtered into the stunned silence. "Not only are they an abomination against nature but also should be scientifically impossible. Where are you even getting the energy to power all of this equipment? We're deep in the jungle here; there aren't any electrical stations around for miles!"

His expression remained bland and indifferent as he studied me from behind the controls. "Nyarlathotep is not the only one who knows how to develop areas of interdimensional space for his own uses. The knowledge of the Brotherhood is extensive, going back hundreds of years, and also includes many aspects of modern-day technology. We utilize energy harnessed from other sources to power this hidden location, all in the name of furthering our plans for a better tomorrow. And now, as you can see, even your companion there has become an integral part of our greater purpose."

At the mention of his involvement, Xavier flinched, tearing his eyes away from the book long enough to gaze about himself in shocked confusion. He suddenly appeared ill, his swarthy features blanching a sickly color as he processed the significance of the priest's words.

"That book he holds contains much knowledge of the so-called forbidden arts," the high priest continued, "including the ritual Nyarlathotep hopes to use to become corporeal. We gain an advantage over him by possessing this tome, but the additional power its pages will provide is also crucial to our success at this juncture. Now that you've involved other players in the game, we'll have to hasten our agenda in order to stay at the forefront of this global tug-of-war you've initiated. Thanks to you, we must race to ensure that our god is the only celestial being left in control once the dust has settled."

Stepping out from behind the control device, his intense gaze bore into me like a raven studying a pile of carrion. "And that brings us to your own contribution," he purred menacingly. "As we discussed earlier, you must now honor your half of the bargain by opening the Mi-Go stronghold."

I did not know what he would do to us once he found out that I didn't actually know how to open a Mi-Go hive. Were we all fated to become minions in his army of modified insectile warriors? I felt a tickle at the edges of my mind, a gentle probing that intensified the more I stood in silent introspection. The link I'd forged with that other space-faring race, the true ancestral enemies of the Mi-Go themselves, was still active. But I had not felt it in such a long while that I'd begun to forget that it was even there.

The last time I'd communicated with that barrel-shaped, extraterrestrial being was while dreaming aboard the transport plane two days ago. My memories of the encounter indicated that the Elder Things we'd released from Mi-Go captivity should all be dead by now. It was obvious that the unknown creature descending upon them in the depths of the Antarctic Ocean had been bent on their destruction. Or, if they had somehow survived its attack, then their own modified servitor race of amoeba-like shoggoths would surely have finished the job. I might have died there as well if it hadn't been for that other mysterious otherworldly presence who'd pulled me back into my own body at the very last second. As my mind shied away from these troubling thoughts, I tried to focus only on what was relevant. How was the link we shared even still active? I had no idea, and suddenly, did not even want to know; the link itself was just another reminder of how badly I'd failed.

Ignoring the insistent probing that called to me from the convoluted corners of my mind, I swallowed my fear and hopelessness, attempting to appear like I still knew what I was doing. The longer I could keep up the charade of having the answers this man sought, the longer we would remain alive. Perhaps one of my companions would come up with a plan of action, yet I did not put much stock in that hope. Sighing inwardly, I chose to stall for more time by engaging the priest in further conversation.

"If we're in a pocket of space like the one that Nathrotep used to house his ghoul hybrid city," I asked, "then how are we in a position to access the Mi-Go base? Surely you aren't saying that the hive is located here on the same grounds as this temple?"

A scream punctuated my question as yet another man was thrown down to feed the Baratusi god in the adjoining room, a stark reminder that these cultists were not the only threat I was dealing with right now. Into the grim silence that followed, the older man spoke.

"You have indeed surmised correctly; we are residing in a place removed from the current reality yet situated within close proximity. My Brotherhood has many ways to traverse the trans-dimensional planes, and we've perfected the ability to use the spaces between them as a sort of pathway into other realms." Motioning his followers to bring us along, he moved across the domed laboratory, approaching the opposite side. Here resided an elaborate archway built into the wall. It was semicircular in design and decorated in the Greek style with fluted columns and finely chiseled bas-reliefs. The air within the archway shimmered, reminding me of the portal we'd come through earlier, yet different in many subtle ways.

"Here is a gateway of sorts," he said, indicating the glimmering vortex within. "We employ this device to travel to other places around the globe."

As he spoke, the swirling veil changed, showing us vistas and glimpses of other environments in an alternating collage of fantastical images. First, a desert landscape at sunset, then ocean waves crashing against a stone pillar. From a field of purple-blue flowers to the darkness of a sunken cavern flooded with water. Many realities flowed past in the space of a heartbeat, showing scene after scene of places I was entirely unfamiliar with. Now a castle on a hill, then a fine dining table set for an elaborate feast, switching to a bedroom decorated like something from the early 1900s. Finally, the images stopped their endless rotation, settling upon a huge doorway in a grotto of stone.

The entrance was immense and shaped like an octagon, its surface covered in sigils and pictographs like the ones we'd encountered in the Brooks Range. Light was directed on this massive portal by a series of construction lamps, giving the impression that it was buried somewhere far below ground. Staring at it in consternation while also struggling to prevent the psychic link from overwhelming my mind, I came to a conclusion.

There was no way that I could open this vault for the Brotherhood of Asklepios. And because of that inadequacy, I might be dooming us all to a life of servitude, possibly as modified minions to this mysterious god known only as Yig.

What other calamitous repercussions was I about to visit upon my unsuspecting comrades? Inwardly, I mourned for them already. Turning my head, I sought to judge their reactions. Ofelia stood glaring at her brother, who, in turn, averted his eyes, clutching the hard-won book as if his very life depended on it. Jarrod was hunched forward, his shoulders drawn in, myopically staring at everything around him as he trembled in uncontrolled terror.

And then, there was Tunuhun.

His rock-solid presence, always a balm to my fraying nerves, was as steadfast as ever. He stood calmly, his body held in loose readiness yet wound tight like a polar bear ready to pounce. Only my intimate knowledge of him allowed me to sense this; the others had no clue that the silent and introspective man was gearing up for fierce brutality. Seeing that he'd caught my eye, he gave me a nod, then made a hand signal I knew only too well: *Be ready.* It told me everything I needed to know without revealing exactly what his intentions might be. But whatever he was preparing to do, I knew that it would not be successful, even if the undead warlock inside him somehow agreed to assist us. We were outnumbered here, surrounded by practitioners of the darkest arts and their army of pet centaurpedes. Returning his nod, I surreptitiously signaled for him to stand down. I had gotten us into this mess; it was my obligation to get us out of it.

There was only one thing I could do. But the very thought of it sent shivers coursing through me, causing a surge of anxiety that I could barely suppress. Yet I was all out of other options. If I didn't do something soon, my lack of knowledge about the hive entrance would surely doom us all. I was forced to place all of my faith, and indeed the chances of our continued survival, on the outcome of this one last desperate gambit.

Centering myself, I settled into a trance-like state, seeking out the connection tethering me to the ancient Elder Thing. Then, wrapping my psyche around this throbbing tendril of alien thoughts and ideas, I embraced it fully, pouring everything I had into the link and allowing my astral form to be engulfed by its foreign perceptions. As my outer semblance remained lightly detached, I forcibly channeled all my spiritual essence directly across this strengthening bond. And as the way opened up before me in a swirl of unfamiliar images and ideology, I shot across the incalculable distances to insinuate myself deeply into the complex five-lobed brain of that star-headed being from another world.

13

The mind of the Elder Thing was unfathomable, and yet we'd shared such a close mental bond that I was beginning to understand its subconscious pathways, recognize the intricacies of its memories and its methods of deduction. Our link, unexpectedly forged in the frigid peaks of the Brooks Range, had grown stronger, and I now used this to my advantage as I strove to break through to the forefront of its conscious perceptions. Weaving my way through its complex alien ideology and convoluted thought patterns, I eventually achieved synchronicity, overlapping its physiology with my own projected mentality.

As our connection solidified, I was surprised to find that it had been trying to contact me for quite some time. Apparently, the Mi-Go hive that the followers of Yig were attempting to enter was vitally important, and it desired nothing more than my overwhelming success at infiltrating its enemy's hidden base. In fact, it cared nothing for the physical dangers I now faced, nor even for the identities of the robed figures who currently surrounded my corporeal body. Instead, it was focused upon one thing only—the information stored within the sealed Mi-Go vault.

But the star-headed lifeform and its companions had been busy since our last joining, which had divided its attention between seeking me out and tending to its own survival. Peering out through its multiple eyestalks, I could view our surroundings in spectra unnatural to the human eye. And in this way, I was able to witness what was going on there in the darkened depths of the Antarctic Ocean.

When I'd inadvertently visited here before, they'd been under attack, surrounded by feral shoggoths as an unknown behemoth descended on them from above. Yet I now saw that those same shoggoths were hard at work rebuilding their vast underwater city. Everywhere within visual range there were stones being raised, ramparts being repaired, and debris being cleared away from structures situated within close proximity to the central plaza. And overseeing it all was the massive creature I'd previously assumed to be a threat.

With a chilling epiphany, I suddenly realized that this monstrous beast was the very same shoggoth who'd fought alongside them within the Mi-Go hive during our escape. I could not believe that it was still alive, having somehow survived the tremendous explosion which had destroyed that prehistoric installation. And it had grown exponentially since then, transforming into a veritable gargantuan, sprouting thousands of unblinking eyes and an endless array of writhing pseudopods. While viewing the immensity of its ever-changing presence, I could feel the Elder Thing's deep appreciation: was that a note of fierce pride that I detected? Could something so alien to our world even have such a human emotion? With our minds so closely linked, a collage of its earliest memories suddenly washed over me, sending me careening through a disjointed history of days long past.

From the images and mental concepts being shared, I was able to ascertain that the Elder Things had come here millions of years ago, seeking asylum from an intergalactic conflict. Finding the Earth uninhabited, they had made it their home, determined to carve out a new life for themselves. But they'd needed help to build their intricate cities, and so they'd engineered a new breed of servitor, a race of protoplasmic beings who could perform all of the manual labor required. This immense shoggoth, the same one who'd attacked the swarms of Mi-Go soldiers during our escape from the Alaskan hive, had been the very first of its kind.

It was ancient, this creation of pseudoscience and genetics. And its wealth of experience and sentient knowledge had allowed it to dominate the rest of the shoggoths around it. Easily their superior in terms of age, growth, and overall intelligence, it was now held in high esteem, a being worthy of their worship and veneration. Thus, the lesser shoggoths had ceased their attack upon the Elder Things, the same hated masters they'd rebelled against thousands of years ago when first seeking freedom from their oppressive enslavement.

And the being I now shared minds with had engineered this original servitor, who in turn was the progenitor of all shoggoths who came after, the wellspring from which all others of its kind had sprung. This gave the Elder Thing a rare supremacy over its comrades while also placing it in charge of the feral shoggoths themselves. So, it had begun the process of rebuilding their fallen aquatic city while also sending out scouts to search for similar locations that may have yet survived. If it could find others of its own kind still living here on Earth, then it would not have to journey through the outer reaches of space in order to locate the long-lost remnants of its far-flung race.

This was one of the main reasons it wanted me to infiltrate the Mi-Go hive in Peru. The technology contained therein would be of great use to it. Not only in helping to find the surviving members of its own species but also in perhaps revealing the locations of its enemy's other hidden strongholds around the globe. Its hatred for the Mi-Go ran deep, like an endless reservoir of festering resentment held barely in check. For they had followed the Elder Things here in those primordial times, bringing with them the continuation of an age-old intergalactic conflict.

As its foreign thought processes recalled this jumble of multifaceted information, it caught itself just on the verge of revealing its innermost desires. Recognizing my presence at last, it swiftly shuttered off that part of its five-lobed brain, pushing me back to the outer fringes of its conscious thoughts. It was apparently unwilling to trust me with its deepest, darkest secrets, at least not yet.

But it did have some very specific information to impart.

Realizing I was sharing more of myself than usual, it seized upon the opportunity, latching onto my consciousness with brutal intensity. There was a key sequence stolen long ago, a way to gain access to Mi-Go outposts that it had discovered on one of its many previous raids. Hundreds of thousands of years ago, when the battle between their two species had raged across the Earth unchecked, it had pilfered this closely guarded secret from the Mi-Go themselves. With dizzying speed, it began to insert these detailed instructions into my brain, initiating a plan that would allow me entry into the sealed Peruvian base. And as I absorbed this data, a part of my astral form that was not unilaterally interwoven within the link suddenly felt the brush of another's questing thoughts.

I did not want to know who this new persona was and wholeheartedly resented their meddlesome interference. I had finally begun to get the guidance needed to open the Mi-Go hive, but here was yet another cosmic entity seeking to overwhelm me with unwanted demands. And even though I recognized their touch upon my mind, they still represented an additional faction that I knew next to nothing about.

On the plane ride to Peru, this powerful being had rescued my astral form from unraveling hundreds of fathoms beneath the waves of the Antarctic Ocean. When my spiritual essence had been accidentally expelled from my bond with the Elder Thing, it had gathered up my fraying consciousness, returning it to my sleeping form. In fact, that experience had taught me much about astral travel, knowledge which I now utilized to my own advantage. But whoever this mysterious new individual was, I decided that I would suffer no further importunities that might divert me from my main objective.

Focusing on the images being fed to me by the Elder Thing, I shut out all other distractions, absorbing and collating the information I would need to open the sealed Mi-Go vault. Then, as the alien I inhabited finished teaching me the key sequence, I began to disconnect myself from our joined identities, preparing to travel back to my own physical form.

But as I was completing the separation, a telepathic probe broke through my paltry defenses. Burrowing through the astral linkage, this unblockable message reverberated painfully within my mind as I sought to follow the connected thread of my spirituality back to the Brotherhood's lab.

"Wait!" the feminine-sounding entreaty boomed out, echoing across the corridors of time and space, "We can help each oth—"

Fortunately, I had already begun my retreat, so I was able to ignore this resonant metaphysical plea. There was enough on my plate right now without adding another deity's demands to the mix. My main goal at the moment was to save my friends, and it was to that end alone that I would now bend my every effort. Perhaps someone else would take up the ongoing struggle to rescue the rest of our world, someone with a better understanding of the threats our planet now faced. For even though I knew that the Earth was now closer to destruction than ever before, I realized in my heart that I was only making things worse the longer I tried to save it.

With a shudder that ran through my entire frame, I flowed back into my own fleshy form, my eyes refocusing on the Brotherhood's transportation device that I'd been silently staring at the entire time. Although it still felt as if I were in a dreamlike state, I began to reconcile myself to being once more physically present. It struck me then, with no small amount of satisfaction, that no one in the room was aware of my recent astral journey. They'd only witnessed what I'd wanted them to see: a man considering a problem that was quite difficult to resolve. Breathing deeply, I attempted to shake off the cloying lethargy. And as I became more aware of my surroundings, I could suddenly sense the high priest's seething anticipation, feel his avid intensity searing into me from behind with an almost palpable impatience.

"Well," he finally demanded. "Can you open it or not?"

I nodded in response, not trusting myself to meet his gaze now that I'd obtained the answer through a connection he still knew nothing about. Studying the sealed Mi-Go door resting beyond the shimmering archway, I began to weave the key elements stored within my mind into cohesive order.

The lock was not a simple one, and to breach its defenses, I would need to overlay a multilayered pattern across its surface by using a telepathic method shown to me by the Elder Thing. In addition to the alien imagery and unfamiliar sigils I was mentally constructing, there was also an audible intonation that must be vocalized at the correct moment, a series of notes and octaves that had not been heard on this planet for eons. At this point, the musical component was a source of some uncertainty. Since singing had never been one of my strong suits, I was unsure that my human vocal cords could even reproduce the required melodies. Still, it would be necessary if I wanted to open the vault's door.

From behind me, there came a chilling scream as the feeding of the Baratusi's divine entity continued in the adjacent room, a shrill cry abruptly cut off as the creature feasted on yet another unwilling sacrifice. Trying my best not to dwell on it, I concentrated on my task, collating the layers I'd formed within my mind into a coherent, three-dimensional image. Sweat was pouring off me now, stinging my eyes and soaking into my clothing as I stood trembling in motionless exertion.

The key was convoluted and uncanny, yet I had sure knowledge of its formation from sharing my intellect with the ancient Elder Thing. Inch by inch, I built up the intricate imagery, fabricating an interconnected set of sigils that I could almost sense as a solid, material object. Much like the Mi-Go data tablets we'd found in the Brooks Range, this complicated design had many layers, each overlapping the last, forming a multileveled cypher. To this envisioned template, I then added the meticulous details required, mentally rotating it within my mind's eye to check for accuracy. When I felt that I'd done all I could, I pushed it outward telepathically, superimposing it across the designs chiseled into the sealed Mi-Go door.

As the convoluted mental construct sank into the stone and aligned itself with the indentations engraved there, I heard an audible 'click.' Assuming that the key had indeed fit, I had only one thing left to do—I had to now somehow reproduce the haunting melody which would activate the mechanism, allowing us entry into its mysterious confines.

But as I prepared to vocalize this series of warbling intonations, there was a sudden disturbance in the room behind me, a sizzling electrical discharge followed by a collective murmur of outrage from the attending acolytes. Turning my head, I was just in time to witness the formation of a swirling vortex materializing in the far corner of the room. Whoever was in charge of that unexpected phenomenon, it appeared that they had somehow followed my astral trail, using me as a focal point to attempt an invasion of the Brotherhood's hidden lair. My attention immediately shifted to the high priest, hoping against all odds that he would not blame this intrusion on me or my associates. We had enough trouble right now without him adding this breach of his security to our long list of other offenses.

Yet he seemed entirely nonplussed. With his expression impassive and unconcerned, he commanded the writhing multitudes of his centaurpedes to form up in a milling tangle in front of the newly opening rift. Tension charged the room with barely suppressed hostility as his orders were carried out. And then, with a near blinding burst of light, glowing figures began flying out of the portal, spreading out to attack the high priest's insectile minions.

They were glorious to behold, these airborne warriors of light and shifting shadow, a luminous squadron of armored assailants resembling knights from the fourteenth century. But their Gothic suits of plate mail were fashioned from brightly colored panes of light instead of steel, a stunning array of rainbow-hued panels like interconnected sheaths of semi-transparent glass. Remaining aloft by some sorcerous means, they struck with a combination of mystical energy blasts and a series of calculated blows from their light-infused medieval weaponry.

This strategy allowed them to rapidly gain the upper hand, decimating huge numbers of opponents at a time. But they could not remain completely unscathed when confronted by such a voracious glut of enraged defenders. Like ants boiling out of a kicked-over nest, the Brotherhood's embattled centaurpedes quickly regrouped, ruthlessly tearing into their adversaries with little regard for their own personal safety. Striking from above, the knights managed to stay airborne for the most part, but the minions of Yig were swift and agile, swarming into towering piles to latch onto their flying foes while also falling from the walls and ceiling to bear them to the ground.

These lab-grown creatures, beings who felt neither fear nor pain, utilized tentacles, pincers, and brawny human musculature to break through their opponent's defenses. With brutal efficiency, they tore limbs from sockets, burst apart armored helms, and wrapped struggling combatants into tightly constricted balls using their long, sinuous bodies. And yet, even while being overwhelmed by superior numbers, the intruders fought on with grim determination. The ensuing struggle inevitably caused tables to be broken and overturned, shattering pieces of scientific apparatus on the floor and filling the air with smoke and acrid fumes as fires broke out across the room.

It was like nothing I'd ever witnessed before, a devastating explosion of violence that soon plastered the walls in a deluge of erupting blood and viscera.

Redoubling their efforts, the armored attackers gradually beat back the centaurpedes, endeavoring to reach me where I stood before the Brotherhood's gateway arch. Glancing toward my companions, I saw that they had hunkered down behind nearby tables, eyeing the ongoing fight with varying degrees of awe and apprehension. And I knew right then that I had to do something fast or we would all be lost, swept away in the rising tide of death and destruction.

But when the high priest realized that I was the main objective of these interlopers, his unexpected reaction shocked me to the core. His austere face, usually a bleak mask of expressionless disdain, snarled like an enraged demon. And this extreme distortion of his pale features caused a series of grotesque ulcerations to split the skin along the edges of his mouth, eyes, and scalp. As blood began to hemorrhage out of these disfiguring rents in his flesh, he cried out in an incomprehensible language before flinging aside his crimson vestments. With a sibilant roar, the rest of his brethren followed suit, discarding their own robes while the light shining down from the stained-glass dome painted them all in shifting, multicolored hues.

With their abhorrent true identities thus exposed, the ill-fitting masks of their borrowed humanity sloughed away in a terrifying glut of peeling, bloodied flesh. And as the shedding of this concealing camouflage uncovered their natural features, sinuously scaled skin was revealed beneath it. Like the Naga out of Asian folklore, these reptilian hybrids had upper bodies sporting humanoid arms while their lower extremities were the limbless coils of immense snakes.

Yet this horrid revelation was not the worst of it, for beyond them in the adjoining room, I could see that the Baratusi tribesmen were now converging on us as well. At the sight of their masters being attacked, they had climbed down through the hole in the ceiling, using thick, resilient vines, their painted and feathered bodies a stark contrast to their ally's startling snake-like appearance. And close behind these fearsome warriors, their loathsome demigod arose from its water-filled cenote, revealing yards of undulating coils topped by a blunt-snouted head.

In mounting despair, I watched as the acolytes of Yig began firing sizzling bolts of lightning from their scaly outstretched palms, electrocuting their armored adversaries with devastating precision. And while those repellent snakemen wove their terrible magic, the immense river serpent slithered through the adjoining archway, power rippling along its slime-coated body in sparkling waves.

The inexorable advance of this electrified ophidian caused an obscure memory to float up from the depths of my panic-crazed mind—what had Xavier said back there on the river when our boat was being attacked by masses of squirming, aquatic creatures? With a flash of insight, everything suddenly became clear to me. The Baratusi godling was, in fact, a gigantic *electrophorus voltai*, the recently discovered new species of eel that was able to discharge a far greater shock than any other member of its kind. And the Brotherhood of Asklepios, being true followers of Yig, the god of snakes, had taken on the abilities of their ally's river-dwelling cryptid, assuming its powers as their own. With this alliance between them, their strength was far greater than I could have ever imagined. Not even the combined might of all the remaining armored invaders could withstand the electricity being generated by that monstrous eel, let alone the ferocity of its demented followers.

Desperately searching for a way out, my eyes locked upon the Mi-Go vault residing just beyond the Brotherhood's transportational archway. Inside its sealed confines, there rested an ancient alien base, perhaps uninhabited for hundreds of thousands of years. But could not a door once opened be locked yet again behind us?

Without wasting another moment, I began to sing the initial notes of the activation trigger, reproducing a melody not heard on this planet since before time began. Within me, the link suddenly flared to life as the Elder Thing provided the mystical support needed to create these unnatural alien sounds, a welcomed joining of its extraterrestrial abilities to my own. And as the octaves of our entwined vocalization rang out across the mental imagery I'd integrated into the Mi-Go door, the diagram chiseled into its rough surface suddenly flared to life. With a discordant chime, the seal was broken, and the huge portal began retracting in a cloud of billowing dust, revealing a darkened tunnel leading down into its shadowy depths.

We would have only a fleeting chance and needed to capitalize on it while our enemies were still distracted. Turning, I signaled to Tunuhun, indicating that we would flee into the hive together. Once inside, I would then seal it shut again behind us. Readying myself, I watched as Tunuhun arose from his crouch, thrusting Ofelia before him as he dragged Jarrod bodily up from the floor by his shirt collar. With my stalwart companion chivying the rest of my team forward, their looming proximity soon forced me to make way, backpedaling toward the glowing archway itself.

But as they stumbled past Xavier, Ofelia flung out her arms, attempting to latch onto her brother and drag him along with us. Lost in thought, he still stood staring down at the forbidden book in his hands, unable or unwilling to even register what was going on around him. Yet as Tunuhun drove her onward, Ofelia's lunging grab missed its mark, catching ahold of the book instead and unintentionally ripping it out of Xavier's grasp.

Coming to his senses with a jolt of surprise, he refocused on Ofelia, his face flushing with anger that quickly turned to heartfelt remorse. Realizing what was happening, he took a tentative step toward us, attempting to follow as we staggered ever closer to the whirling vortex of the Brotherhood's transportation device.

Then something truly strange happened, an unexpected event that I could scarcely credit. As I watched on in growing disbelief, a small, furry creature darted between the struggling combatants in the room, zig-zagging its way across the bloody field of battle at breakneck speed. Jumping onto the table next to Xavier, it made a prodigious leap, a tremendous display of feline skill and agility. As it flew past me, the trans-dimensional gateway giving access to the Mi-Go hive reconfigured to another destination entirely. Changing from an image of the opening Mi-Go vault, it shifted back to a room it had displayed earlier, an unknown location featuring resplendent Victorian décor. As the rest of my team slammed into me, we were caught in a tangle of flailing limbs, collapsing through the portal together to sprawl painfully onto a solid hardwood floor.

I wanted to believe this was all a mistake, some sort of mad fever dream, but the smarting pain in my elbows and knees, the smell of wood smoke in the air, convinced me otherwise. Suffering vertigo from our translocation, I muzzily came to grips with the fact that we were not inside the ancient Mi-Go base as I'd originally planned. And as I fought back against the wooziness and trembling shock of our arrival, I wondered if we'd ever be able to reenter the Brotherhood's hidden laboratory to make a second attempt. But upon glancing back, I found that the trans-dimensional gateway was now gone, replaced by a large, ornate mirror. In mute despair, I watched as its sparkling surface rapidly transformed to display nothing more than the reflection of my companions and I where we lay sprawled across the floor of this eerily lit room.

The cat, having landed on its feet, ran forward to jump into the lap of a woman resting comfortably in a rocking chair sitting next to a crackling fireplace. "Mr. Tibbets!" she exclaimed, burying her face in the cat's fur for a moment before looking up at us. "You naughty thing! What have you broughten us this time?"

With a rumbling purr, the cat glanced back over one shoulder, its fathomless eyes glowing in the flickering firelight, and I was overcome by a surge of emotion. It was a safe bet that we were no longer in Peru and that the Mi-Go stronghold located there was forever lost to us. Its secrets were now most likely in the hands of the Brotherhood of Asklepios. Or perhaps the ancient base had even been captured by whoever those armored vigilantes were working for, depending on the outcome of the battle. In any event, it no longer mattered—my failure had damned us all.

The woman smiled, her pink-tinged eyes studying us shrewdly, and I realized that she was an albino. Dressed in multicolored skirts, she represented an unknown aspect, a new wrinkle in the fabric of our quest, forced upon us by the vicarious nature of a wayward cat. But whoever she may be, wherever we were right now, I knew that our mission was at an end. All the hardships we'd thus far endured, the obstacles we'd overcome, our trials and tribulations leading up to this point, all of it had become utterly invalid. Lowering my head to the hard wooden floorboards, I wept, losing control of myself in the face of such a total loss.

I did not know where we would go from here, but I was almost beyond caring. The Earth and all its inhabitants were surely doomed to destruction by my incompetence.

And I was powerless to prevent it . . .

ABOUT THE AUTHOR

William H. Nelson grew up in Anchorage, Alaska, where he attended college at UAA. During his time there, he was a regular contributor to several publications, including, The Radical (Radical Publications, 1992–94), The Auroran (Denali Publications 1993–96), and Rainsongs (Denali Publications 1995–96). 

After moving to the Seattle area in 1998, he eventually met the love of his life, and they now reside in a small town just across the bay from the Emerald City. Although William continues to write every day, in his spare time he also enjoys reading voraciously, playing the drums like a berserk spider monkey, creating award-winning costumes and props for local conventions, watching movies with a passion bordering on obsession, and playing selections from his vast collection of truly epic fantasy board games.

Connect with William on Facebook!
www.facebook.com/williamhnelsonbooks

Official Website:
www.williamhnelsonbooks.com